PROTOCOL FOR MURDER

by
PAUL NATHAN

THE PERMANENT PRESS
Sag Harbor, New York 11963

THE PERMANENT PRESS
Noyac Road
Sag Harbor, NY 11963

For Ruth, with love

ONE

Just when smart people were deciding they'd had it with New York, I was listening to its siren song. My old friend from the days when we both wrote for the *New York Record*, Hazel Claflin, had called this morning and said, "There's an opening here in P.R. at the Krinsky Research Center. Your title would be Director of Media Relations. How about flying up for an interview?"

In the half dozen years since the *Record* had folded and I'd gone south, New York had been sliding closer to disaster. Kids were shooting each other in the schools or setting the homeless on fire, AIDS victims jammed the hospitals, potholes and drug addicts proliferated, corporations took off for gentler climes and lower taxes, hitmen and madmen roamed the streets.

From where I was sitting New York looked good.

At the moment I was half-turned from my computer, glaring out at Florida's most hated palm tree. Why would anyone hate a palm tree? If you don't like living in Florida, it's easy—and this particular tree happened to be smack in the center of my office window. It was *always* there—a constant reminder of what I'd settled for in life: blue skies, sand in my shoes and high pay for grinding out tripe for a supermarket tabloid.

The story struggling to be born on my monitor was about poltergeists; *Inside Story* had been neglecting them lately and had sent me to Pottsville, Pa., to report on the hi-jinks of one of the little nasties. Nothing had occurred while I was there, but the Previt family did include the requisite adolescent—a sulky boy of fourteen (poltergeist experts believe adolescents set off the manifestations). A cracked mirror over the mantel and scarred dining room furniture were said to have been hit by a flying floor lamp, itself banged up. Neighbors who came to check me out confirmed that on previous visits they'd heard strange tappings in the walls.

Now, seated before my computer keyboard, I was trying to make something out of very little for dimbulb readers. The fact was, however, that my mind wasn't on poltergeists; it was playing with the possibility that I could quit my present idiotic employment for something high class in the Big, if rotting, Apple. According to Hazel, the P.R. job was suddenly available because the previous incumbent had just gotten the boot. She'd tell me why when she saw me.

Hazel was a very busy lady these days. She was Development Director for Westside General Hospital, with which the Krinsky Research Center was affiliated. Hospital and center were jointly engaged in a hundred-million-dollar building fund campaign.

"It sounds great," I'd said when she explained what she had in mind for me, "but my résumé—"

"What's wrong with your résumé? And incidentally, when you present your credentials in the world of medical science, you don't call it a résumé. It's a c.v."

"Curriculum vitae. I know. What's wrong with it is *Inside Story*. What kind of background is this for the top P.R. spot in a world-famous research facility?"

"How long have you been with The Junk Journal?"

I did a quick calculation. "Year and a half next month."

"When you put the c.v. together make it a year and a half of freelancing. Nobody has to know."

"But before that I was four years on *Physicians Quarterly*. A nothing publication."

"I've seen it—bought and paid for by the drug companies. It doesn't matter. You're a top medical science writer with terrific media connections."

"Who says?"

"I do."

I paused. Maybe it should have been a longer pause . . . permanent. "How's the money?"

"Negotiable, but I'm sure at least as good as you're making."

I had to pay attention to that. I was the main support of my eleven-year-old daughter living with her mother in Toronto. If it hadn't been for my responsibility to Paula, I probably never would have gone to work for *Inside Story* after being fired from *Physicians Quarterly* for calling the editor a ball-less wonder. He'd refused to print my exposé on a chain of hospitals run by doctors who were cooking the books and gypping the IRS. I'd known he would. I was itching to quit but wanted to force him to terminate me so I could collect unemployment insurance while I looked for a situation more suited to my talents.

And where did I end up? The Junk Journal, as Hazel so aptly put it.

"When shall I plan to come?"

"I'll ask Cromart to set a date. He's the center director."

"I hope you know what you're doing," I said. "I could be the second Director of Media Relations to end up out on my ass."

"If you make me look bad I'll kill you."

I was at one of those moments when you're forced to take stock of your life. How did I get here, where am I headed? What I'd accomplished by age forty-seven wasn't too impressive. Decreasing job satisfaction. Failed marriage, followed by meaningless affairs. It was hard to remember now that Doreen and I once had fun together. She was pursuing a career then in ballet; I was a reporter—a legitimate one. As it happened, I too liked to dance—ballroom style, to Goodman, Basie, Crosby, Ella et al. on the record player. I was even pretty good at it. The times I coaxed my wife into my arms, to lead her in fancy twirls and dips, may have been the best part of our marriage—for me.

We gave it up after Paula arrived. At two and a half she would show her displeasure when we took to the floor, forcing herself between our legs until we quit. Baby jealousy. Doreen may have been glad to call a halt; my kind of terpsichore was something she condescended to.

Well, no percentage in revisiting old regrets and resentments. I had this damn story to get out of my computer. And after that, a chance to gain back some of my professional self-respect in a new set of circumstances.

Hazel called back the next day, and at ten-thirty a.m. a week later I was in her office in Westside General Hospital.

This lady had never been beautiful or even pretty, but her face was a map of intelligence and humor. When I joined the *Record* she'd been in the midst of a hot affair with a TV reporter, and although I suspect it was real love on her part she survived the eventual breakup unembittered. By the time my own marriage collapsed Hazel had pitched a tent with somebody else, otherwise I might have gone for her myself. Today, both of us without any serious attachment, we were comfortable in a friendship where sex had been factored out.

My appointment with Dr. John Cromart, the man I'd be trying to sell myself to, was set for eleven.

I said, "Tell me what I have to know before I meet him."

"I'm going to. I like your suit." I was wearing my tropical pinstripe executive navy blue, reserved for summer life or death occasions.

"The first thing I want to know," I prompted, "is what happened to whoever had the job I'm looking at."

"Head of the purchasing department at Krinsky was inflating the bills on lab equipment and supplies and pocketing the overcharges. Been getting away with it for a long time. A new comptroller took over, discovered what was going on and fired him. It was supposed to be hushed up so the big givers on the board wouldn't know the center's bookkeeping was less than perfect. Unfortunately there was a leak—press and TV jumped in and your predecessor got bumped for not being able to control the damage."

"I'm not sure I could've done any better."

"That wasn't the first time he'd screwed up. All things being equal, you shouldn't have to deal with any messes for quite a while, and you do have pals in the press."

"I don't know how many are left."

"Stop being honest! Now let me draw you a plan of organization—you'll see where you fit in."

She put pen to yellow pad and in a minute tore off the sheet and handed it to me:

WESTSIDE MEDICAL CENTER

Westside General Hospital	⟷	Krinsky Research Center
Director: T Graydon Stokes, M.D.		Director: John Cromart, Ph.D.
(Responsible to Board of Governors)		(Reports to Board of Trustees)

Director, Media Relations: <u>You?</u>

↓

Westside General is Teaching
Hospital for
<u>Manhattan Medical College</u>

"Got the picture," I said.

"You notice the two-way arrow between hospital and Krinsky. They cooperate."

"Does the hospital have its own P.R. director?"

"Yes, but he'll keep out of your hair. You know what goes on in Krinsky?"

I had a pretty good general idea; it used to be part of my beat when I was with the *Record*. "Molecular biology. Genetic engineering. Cancer ... tropical diseases ... I suppose AIDS."

"Definitely AIDS. And there's a new leprosy project. All sorts of things."

"Leprosy? Is Hansen's disease a problem in this country?"

"It's getting to be. Immigrants ... from the Third World." She moved to the next topic. "Now, about our building fund campaign. The hospital and Krinsky both need more space."

"Hundred million bucks you said. How's it going?"

"Not bad. But there's community opposition, you'll run into some of that."

"What are they objecting to?"

"The new construction will cut off light and air, block views, bring more traffic, noise and pollution."

"How about the fact that a bigger hospital and research center should improve people's health?"

"Fine, as long as it's NIMBY—not in my back yard."

"Okay, what else do I have to know?"

"Cromart. He's not the easiest person to get along with. I hear the head of one lab may be planning to leave on account of him."

"Thanks a lot," I said, "for saving the good news until I got here."

9

"Oh, you can handle him. By the way, we call him Darryl. Behind his back."

"Why is that?"

"You'll see. Okay, let's go." She stood.

From her first-floor office she walked me down the hall and, after a couple of turns, into a long corridor that connected the hospital with the Krinsky building. We became part of a small flow of traffic. Emerging at the far end, we made our way to a bank of elevators and took one up to the seventh floor. Here we stepped out into a sleek designer world. A carved black lacquer Chinese table held an oversize crystal vase containing at least two dozen silvery-pink roses. Underfoot was a springy light-gray broadloom that matched walls lined with vibrant prints, the artists identified for me as we passed: Diebenkorn, Motherwell, Rivers, and other contemporary Americans.

"Cromart demands the best—for himself," said Hazel.

She led me the length of the hall to the last door where we were greeted by a stylish secretary, then ushered into a large, walnut-paneled corner office. Dr. John Cromart was seated behind a partners' desk of imposing proportions; behind him, sunlight poured in through windows curtained with the sheerest of white net.

"Here's your man," Hazel introduced me. "Bertram Swain, ace medical science reporter and P.R. whiz. Bert, Dr. Cromart." With a nod my way: "See you later."

"Thank you, Ms. Claflin." As she left, the center director came round the desk, hand outstretched. "That's quite a buildup. Have a seat."

I chose one of two matching period armchairs. We sized each other up discreetly. Cromart had silver hair, neatly parted at the side and shining as though freshly shampooed. A narrow mustache accented the straight line of his mouth. His eyes were light, cool. He wore a suit that looked like the finest silk.

"So you want to be Director of Media Relations," he said. "Why?"

"Several reasons. I covered medical science for the old *Record* and I developed a lot of respect for Krinsky. I also made friends with other people on the beat. Most of 'em are still

10

around . . . good contacts. I can keep my cool in rough situations. I have a few markers I can call in if I have to. [Not true, but I was taking Hazel's advice re honesty.] I've gone on reporting research since I left New York; what I don't know I can pick up. I'd consider it an honor to be working here and I'll guarantee to do the kind of job you people deserve."

Cromart got to his feet and I wondered what kind of pronouncement he had to deliver that required standing. But saying nothing, he walked along the windowed wall behind him to the corner. There rested a golf bag, out of which he plucked a club. I wouldn't know a brassie from a niblick, but whatever it was, he carried it into the middle of the room, stopped, assumed a stance and took a swing. Hazel's "We call him Darryl" came into my head. I remembered that when Darryl Zanuck was head of 20th Century-Fox he'd been famous for conducting polo practice in his office. Meant, no doubt, to remind the underlings that they were not the most important thing on his mind.

After a few more swings, Cromart left off. "I've read your c.v. and taken a look at *Physicians Quarterly*. Hazel says there's no need to check your references—she'll vouch for you. Wish I had a woman who'd go to the mat for me like that. How much money are we talking about?"

I told him what I wanted, he told me what they could pay, which was more than I'd hoped to get. We set a starting date, two weeks from next Monday.

Now I'd have to do things like give notice, find a mover, pack, decide whether to sell or keep my Camry (a questionable asset in Manhattan) and say goodbye to my girlfriends, Miriam and Brenda. I was going to miss their cooking. And their beds. I'd miss Carolyn, too, though she was more of a fallback—a terrible cook.

Maybe there was something to be said for Florida after all. Well, too bad, fella—it's a little late in the day for that.

I sold the car the day before I left and arrived in New York feeling like a kid just starting school. Dear Hazel, with all she had to keep her hopping, had made time to check on possible apartments. Only one within my price range measured up to her standards. A quick look and I took it. It was on East Fifty-first Street on the second floor of an elevator building with doorman; one bedroom, a small neat kitchen, nearly adequate closets and a view of the street. It was actually more than I could afford, but if I avoided restaurants, the theater, female companionship, drinking, buying clothes, buying *anything*, I should be able to skin by. I reminded myself that money is flexible. In the days when Doreen and I were trying to work out our differences by going to psychiatrists, we never had any money yet managed to eat, keep Paula decent and take in an occasional movie.

When I saw my new office in Krinsky I had a twinge of nostalgia for the hated palm tree. The window gave onto a courtyard that served as a delivery area. A truck was unloading metal tanks as I looked down four floors. On the windowsill were a couple of uninspiring plants of the sort that don't require much light and never flower but do have to be watered sometimes and hadn't been lately. Hazel, inspecting the office with me, said to throw those out and she'd replace them. Housewarming present.

A secretary, assigned to me blind, came in as we were leaving. She was a diminutive, olive-skinned young woman: Altagracia Rosario. As I was to discover, I couldn't have done better if I'd hand-picked her.

I spent the next few days going from lab to lab, meeting the center cast of characters and asking what they were working on. In one lab I fell head over heels in lust with a lovely young blond, name of Beth Martin. You'd think at my time of life a man would have simmered down about women, and as a matter of fact it was different in Florida where I had settled arrangements. Here in New York I had yet to find myself even one girl. A couple of sallies to singles bars had provided take-out sex, but I disliked singles bars—especially in the age of AIDS when caution chilled attraction. I wanted something better, a relationship.

Beth Martin, unfortunately, was not for me. That's what I told myself. She was too young—mid twenties at the most—and deserved to be with good-looking, energetic young guys. I resolved to put her out of my mind.

Much of what the lab workers said they were doing was over my head. Like the complicated method by which someone was trying to purify and decipher a substance put out by tumor cells—a protein that suppresses the ability of the immune system to fight the tumor. Or another researcher's technique for using monoclonal antibodies to learn how body cells respond to signals that announce the presence of infection. I promised myself that if and when such studies produced newsworthy information, I'd go back and get them explained again—and again—until *I* could explain them to science writers.

I phoned those I used to know from my *Record* days, taking the ol' buddy approach. I let them know I was now at Krinsky, ready to answer questions and arrange interviews with investigators. No one was wildly interested. Then, to prove to my boss that I was a self-starter, I came up with the idea of a monthly newsletter. It would report on projects under way, papers by our researchers appearing in journals, and so on. This would require a budget for printing and mailing, but I figured Cromart would approve and give the go-ahead.

"We're trying to contain costs not add to them," he said sourly when I'd stated my case.

"It should pay for itself," I argued. "Our contributors will see what their money is doing and give more."

"We're already putting the squeeze on them for the building fund!" What kind of a dolt was I to want to divert money from that? He emphasized my stupidity with a swipe of his niblick (?).

"You can handle him," Hazel had said. Ha.

My first crisis came in my second week. Hazel had mentioned that one of the lab heads might quit, and he did, taking his Nobel in physiology with him to a new job in Seattle. The delighted University of Washington School of Medicine trumpeted its coup, and immediately I was getting calls: Why was Dr. Philip Etcheverry decamping?

As soon as I'd learned Etcheverry was leaving, I'd gone to see him and persuaded him not to go public with his reasons—which had to do with Cromart. He'd agreed I could tell anyone who asked that he was making the move primarily to be near his son, who lived in Spokane. If cornered by reporters, he would back me up.

I had begun to lull the suspicions of my callers when POW! Copies of a petition signed by Etcheverry's colleagues fell into media hands. Addressed to Cromart with cc's to the center trustees, the complaint charged the director with responsibility for Etcheverry's resignation. It went on to list such gripes as his arbitrary policy decisions, his inaccessibility, his lack of leadership in a recruitment program for promising young scientists and his too-frequent attendance at conferences next door to golf courses.

Now the situation was beyond my control and word of it got into print and on the air.

Fortunately, most of the people I'd misled about Etcheverry's motivation realized that in my shoes they would have done the same. If they weren't likely to believe everything I told them from now on, at least they could continue to respect my professionalism.

Cromart, forced on the defensive by the protest, had to enlist me as an ally. With my advice and help he drew up a statement promising reforms. After this gesture of good will, outside interest in the troubles at Krinsky faded. There were other, more exciting, scabrous and gruesome stories elsewhere to feed the public's appetite. I knew, and Cromart knew I knew, that any actual improvements would fall short of what he'd guaranteed.

In the meantime I'd done the job I was being paid to do. And, as lagniappe, won Cromart's permission to publish my newsletter. The first one came out and was a hit.

One Tuesday morning in June I was called to Dr. Ralph Wells's office. He headed one of the labs and I'd met him on my getting-acquainted tour. It was in his lab, incidentally, that I'd set eyes on Beth Martin. I looked for her now through an open doorway I passed, but she was not in my line of vision.

Wells was an informal sort—tieless, jacketless—and his office was unpretentious. Heavy-rimmed glasses rested halfway down his nose, but not in an old-fogey professorial way. The nose was decisive, and the set of the glasses gave you the sense that they were a tolerated nuisance. Wells's skin had good outdoor color; he wore his curly brown hair short.

"I guess you're our troubleshooter around here," he began

14

as soon as we were seated, "and we seem to have a problem on our hands."

My heart sank. I'd already had a taste of problems, enough to last me for a while, and here we were again. So much for Hazel's prediction that I wouldn't have any messes to deal with for the foreseeable future. Her batting average was declining precipitously.

"Hopefully," Wells went on, "our little puzzle will solve itself in the next day or two—but if it doesn't, Krinsky doesn't need more bad press. If you know what I mean."

I owned that I did and inquired as to the nature of the puzzle.

"Yesterday one of my staff didn't show up—Faith Frawley. It happened I wasn't here . . . I occasionally take Mondays off in the summer, to work around my place in the country, so I didn't hear about it till this morning. Faith's been with me for years, solid as a rock, and she's never been absent without notice. Naturally, I was concerned, so I asked Gordon Barnard—he's the junior investigator on a project with her—to see what he could find out. He'd already tried to reach her on the phone. Now he's just back from Roosevelt Island—that's where she lives. Excuse me." Wells's secretary had just announced through the open door, "Sergeant Brenner."

Wells picked up his phone. "Yes, sergeant. . . . What! That's wonderful. How did it—. . . I see. . . . I see. I can't thank you enough." There was a rather long pause, then he said, "No. No, that isn't mine. He got that somewhere else. . . . Well, I guess it was easier for him to lie, to say it was all from the same place. . . . Yes, I'll drop around later to pick them up. And please thank the officers who . . . Oh, probably early this afternoon, as soon as I can make time. Thanks again."

Replacing the handset in the cradle, he turned to me. "I'm in luck! Incredibly lucky in fact. I did something dumb last night—left my car parked in the street while I went into a coffee shop. I was only going to be about ten minutes, the street was brightly lit, it would have taken me as long to park in a garage and walk back as to sit at the counter and have a sandwich and coffee. So I took a chance—and in just a few minutes somebody stole my radio; but what's worse, they broke into the trunk and took a pair of candlesticks—Georgian, over two hundred years old. Some work was supposed to be done on them—a damnfool maid put them in the dishwasher, can you believe that? Anyway, I didn't know how I was going to tell the wife—but here they've been found!"

"That's great!" I managed to get in before he rushed on: "It seems the police have been keeping an eye on a certain fence and when the thief walked in with the stuff I'd just reported, they nabbed him."

"Usually you don't get things back," I said.

"I know, I never expected to. And I was kicking myself for bringing the car into town. Normally, I'd leave a wagon or the Jeep at the station in Mt. Kisco to be waiting for me when I get off the train on Fridays, but this time I had those candlesticks to take to Brooklyn. That's where the fixit man lives—Brighton Beach of all places, he's a Russian, part of that colony. It's pretty far out, so I thought the easiest thing was to drive. Well, I'm boring you with a long story. . . ."

"No, and I don't blame you for feeling good about it."

Settling down to business again, he said, "I was telling you about Gordon Barnard. Did you meet him when you were in here before?"

"I don't remember him by name, but I might recognize him."

"Well, I'll introduce you. Anyway, he went over to Roosevelt Island, to Faith's building, and rang her bell. No answer, so he located the super and explained the situation. Super fetches keys, they go into the apartment together and look around. No sign of our girl—no sign of anything wrong. Frankly, Swain, I'm worried. It's not like Faith, not like her at all."

"You don't think the police should be notified?"

"I think if you call them so soon when someone doesn't show up, they don't take it seriously. But I take it seriously, knowing how unlike Faith it is. And if there's a chance to resolve this without the cops—without the publicity . . ." He removed his glasses, blew to remove something from one of the lenses (so, evidently, he did look through them, even at half mast on his nose), . . . put them back on. His next remark was illogical, given the legitimate concern he'd just expresssed: "I can't help feeling she'll turn up with a perfectly good excuse."

"I'll see what I can find out. I'll try to talk to her neighbors—maybe someone spoke to her over the weekend. Was there anything worrying her, do you know? She might have wanted to go someplace, think things over."

He gave the question his consideration. "I don't know what she would have had to worry about." He stood. "Take a look here."

I got up and joined him in front of a picture on the wall. It was an enlargement of a color photo shot by someone on one side of an outdoor swimming pool showing a group of people on the other. Several were in the water, the rest were sitting on the edge dangling their feet in.

"Is this your lab crew?"

He nodded. "Fourth of July five years ago up at my place. This is Faith." I moved closer to see where he was pointing. She was one of those seated. I now recalled having met her in the lab. Hers was a broad face, strong; she wore her straight light-brown hair in bangs across her forehead, jaw length at the sides. In the picture her eyes were an arresting feature. They gazed out steadily and there seemed to be a kind of eagerness about them to take things in. You might say it was the way a scientist's eyes ought to look. Another thing that struck me as I stood there was the wideness of her hips. She was not corpulent, but she was rather big. It was a womanly wideness suggesting she was built for motherhood.

Interesting: the eyes of the Faith Frawley I'd met a few weeks ago lacked the quality of engagement I was seeing here. And dressed in white lab coat over a nondescript dress, she had appeared not womanly so much as heavy. Which of the impressions she gave was truer I had no way of knowing. Maybe on her day in the country she was carefree, in high spirits—not her usual self. Or if it was her usual self, that had been five years ago, and it might not be any more.

One other person I recognized was a young Japanese woman, in the pool, wearing a bathing cap. Wells was not visible, in or out. As I surmised, he had taken the picture.

"Well, now I know who I'm looking for," I said. "I'll go

this afternoon around five, when people'll start getting home from work."

"Thanks, I appreciate it. I'll introduce you to Gordon Barnard." He moved toward the door.

I followed. "Is it Doctor Barnard?"

"Yes. Ph.D."

He walked me into a good-sized, airy room filled with the various machines, jugs, jars, reference books and contraptions of the typical research laboratory. Heavily loaded shelves ran almost all the way to the ceiling. Four people, absorbed in their tasks, were standing or sitting at the Formica-topped benches that extended most of the way across the floor. One of them was Beth! My heart did a flipflop. Fool! I cursed myself. You know she's off limits.

Thanks to her presence, I didn't see anyone else—really see them—although I'd counted the other bodies. I was aware of a radio tuned low to a rock station.

Leaving this room, we entered another, almost identical to it. Here, there were three people. I recognized the Japanese woman, little more than a girl to judge by her appearance, but having been with Wells at least five years she must have been older than she looked. Of the two men in this section Wells steered me to a well-set-up fellow, perhaps in his early thirties, with sunstreaked light-brown hair. I didn't remember him and figured he'd probably been out the day I breezed through.

"I told you about Mr. Swain," Wells said to Barnard, introducing us.

"Yes, Ralph said he hoped you'd be able to help us. I didn't find out anything today when I went over to Roosevelt Island. Have you met Faith?"

"Briefly. I went around to all the labs when I started this job. I didn't meet you, though."

"Well, now that you have . . . if there's anything I can tell you . . . She and I've been working together on this study for over a year. She's brilliant."

"I'll leave you gentlemen," said Wells.

Barnard offered me a near-by chair—they were tall, like bar stools—and resumed his seat.

I said, "I've never been over to Roosevelt Island. You pick

up that sky car on Second Avenue and Fifty-ninth, am I right?"

"Yes. Just a couple of minutes from Manhattan and you're suddenly in a small town."

"What building is she in and how do I get to it . . . and find the super?"

He supplied the information, repeated what he'd said to Wells about the apartment appearing undisturbed and wished me better luck then he'd had.

I lingered. "Is it going to be hard for you to finish what you're working on if your partner never gets back?"

Never gets back! The idea seemed to jolt him. I'd discovered as a reporter that if you startle people they sometimes say things they didn't mean to—maybe things they didn't even know they knew or thought. All Barnard said, however, was, "Gee! Faith never getting back? I'm not ready to deal with that! Not at this point.

"I'd certainly miss her," he added after a moment, "and probably waste time trying things she'd wouldn't bother with. She's had a lot more experience than me. Luckily, the first part of our study's in the bag; we have our results, they're going to be published in *Cell*."

"You have to have something pretty damn good to get in there."

He smiled, with some satisfaction. "It'll be the next round where it hurts—if she didn't come back. But she will!"

While I was walking down the hall a minute later, someone tapped my arm. I stopped. The Japanese woman had followed me. She was very attractive, features and coloring both delicate, dark eyes large in her oval face. She was of medium height and wore her black hair in a sort of gamine cut.

"Before you get away . . ." she said in unaccented English. (It should have been—she was born in Washington, D.C., I learned later.)

"Yes?"

"I heard what you were saying, and maybe I can be of help."

"Should we go somewhere to talk?"

"I'm cloning something—I can't take more than a minute." We moved closer to the wall so people could pass. "I'm a friend of Faith's—I know her away from the lab. We're not all that close . . . she's not an easy person to get next to . . . but we visit back and forth, do things together. Only, the last year or so she's changed."

"In what way?"

"She's more distant. It's like she's been going through something."

"You have any idea . . . ?"

"Last Friday she said she was planning a showdown with her boyfriend over the weekend."

"Who's her boyfriend?"

"She always kept that part of her life private."

"Well, did she indicate what the showdown was about?"

"She was fed up. That's all she'd say. After things were settled she was going to tell me who the man was—she said I'd be surprised. I called her Sunday to ask if it had come off. I hoped it would change things and she'd be happier and we could be friendlier again."

"You called . . . and was there an answer?"

She shook her head no. "I tried twice, and once again yesterday. I'm wondering if they might have gone off some place together."

"You mean the showdown would have been successful."

"Yes and they've patched things up. I hope that's it! By the way, my name's Fumi Tashamira. We met before when you came to the lab." She offered her hand; it was small and firm.

"I remember. Dr.—is it *Dr.* Tashamira?" She nodded. "I have an idea. You've been in Dr. Frawley's apartment—more than once it sounds like."

"Oh yes, many times."

"You know what's supposed to be there, how she kept things. Dr. Barnard said nothing was disturbed, but he might not have noticed—I don't even know if this was his first visit."

"No, he was there once when I was."

"Well, do you think you could join me when I go take a look this afternoon?"

"I'd be glad to. Where shall we meet?"

We agreed on downstairs in the lobby.

TWO

In the sleeveless flowered summer dress that had been concealed by her lab smock, Dr. Tashamira looked even more girlish than before, so when she asked me please to call her Fumi it was easy to oblige. She was to call me Bert.

We took a cab crosstown to the tram station where we climbed two flights to the landing. A dozen passengers were already aboard the waiting gondola. Joining them, we found the built-in benches, fore and aft, pretty much filled. This being a first trip for me, I preferred to stand anyway and see as much as I could through the windows.

Looming immediately on the right was the bridge to Queens, alongside which our cables were strung. Vehicles were streaming across the bridge's cantilevered web of steelwork. Also on the right, apartment towers competed for light and air, reminding me of the *casus belli* of opponents of West-side Medical Center's expansion program. On the opposite side, to the north, buildings were lower, showing more blue sky. In both directions one could follow Second Avenue's long lines of southbound traffic, stopping and starting as lights changed. A sudden firetruck heading downtown in a blare of ear-splitting noise bulled its way through cars driving bumper to bumper.

Fumi and I moved to the front windows. A short distance ahead lay the East River and, in the middle of it, the island. Soon, with a young woman in uniform at the controls, our capsule started gliding upward and forward. Quickly we reached the river's edge; sailing over, we caught a fleeting glimpse of boats, cut off as we descended to the covered terminal which, on this end, was at ground level.

Disembarking and walking out into the open, I had the

Paul Nathan

feeling of having left city limits. While Manhattan rose directly before us, it seemed to have nothing to do with this little piece of land. Some of our fellow passengers went from the tram to a waiting minibus; Fumi led me to the right on a curving sidewalk toward a cluster of squarish red-brick apartment buildings some distance away.

En route, one old white frame house set back on a tree-shaded lawn spoke of a time when there might have been a farm here. A handful of other walkers, a plumber's truck and a second minibus, slow-moving, coming toward us, evoked a sense of small town. I asked Fumi how the truck with a Long Island address and phone number on the panel had got out here.

"There's a bridge from Queens." That would be on the far side from where we were.

A sign on the main street, when we reached it, said Main Street. A car with an elderly man at the wheel, two women out together pushing strollers in the warm, humid air, a couple of shops and an office suggested that if this prepackaged community had a nerve center, this was probably it.

What was missing was the randomness, the unexpected juxtapositions of architecture, people, colors, odors, that gave life to the anthill we had left behind.

Set off in a small plaza, a church, darker than the structures around it and with distinctive stonework, broke the general monotony, but monotony remained the rule. Even the view of the larger island across the water did not include its more spectacular skyscrapers. Except for the neo-Gothic piles of New York Hospital-Cornell Medical Center, most of the big buildings visible from here were just big buildings. No Empire State, no Woolworth, no Chrysler, no World Trade or Rockefeller Center, not even the Chippendale-crested SONY (originally AT&T) oddity.

Why did I feel that if I lived here in synthetic suburbia I'd be getting shortchanged on the view? Did I see something so great through my windows on Fifty-first Street?

Soon Fumi came to a stop in front of an apartment house. "This is it."

We climbed the few steps to the glass doors and entered the lobby. In the space leading to a second pair of doors we located the panel with tenants' names and apartment numbers. There was also a buzzer for J.A. Arco, Supt., and I pressed it. A voice rasped through the intercom: "Yeah?"

"We need to see you about one of your tenants."

"Which one?"

"Dr. Frawley."

A pause, then: "Somebody already been here 'bout her."

"I know. But I've brought a friend of Dr. Frawley's. We have to get into her apartment."

"Jes' a minute."

It being cooler in the lobby than outside, the wait was not unpleasant. One of the interior glass doors opened and Arco emerged, a short, black-haired, dark-eyed man with a late-afternoon stubble. I handed him my business card and explained that we worked with Dr. Frawley and were concerned about her absence. We knew Dr. Barnard had been through her apartment earlier today, but Dr. Tashamira, as a frequent visitor, would have a better idea what to look for.

Arco eyed us dubiously. "Something happen to 'er, huh?"

"We hope not," I said. "Maybe she's just taking some time off. But it's funny she didn't tell somebody."

"Why you not call police?"

"Maybe we will. But first we have to be sure there's really something wrong."

He scowled. "There *is* something wrong, then police not like it I let people in and they move things around, spoil fingerprints . . ."

I reached for my wallet. "Look, we won't touch a thing. And if there's any blame, I'll take the heat." I pressed a twenty on him.

It met no resistance. He had, as it turned out, brought the keys with him. A couple of minutes later we were in Faith's top-floor apartment, Arco standing by to see that we didn't steal anything. Foyer . . . living room . . . it was rather like my place—only with a slice of that view I'd been so cavalier about. Furnishings were plain; prettification clearly did not interest the person who resided here.

A window was open a few inches. With the air conditioning off, we were uncomfortably aware of the weather.

As we started a slow tour my eye was caught by a sideboard in the living room on which stood four highball glasses, four wine glasses, a shot glass and a bottle of whiskey. If this was supposed to be a bar, it was a skimpy one. I asked Fumi if one bottle was all Faith generally kept on hand.

"Oh, she doesn't touch alcohol. The first time I was here to dinner she had wine, but I made her promise not to buy it again just for me."

"Then who's the hard stuff for?"

"I don't know."

Maybe for the boyfriend. I examined the label: Tullamore Dew, Irish. I was partial to Irish whiskey myself, but this was a brand I'd never heard of.

Then something struck Fumi. She'd come to a stop before a bookcase. "There used to be a pair of bookends here." Eight or nine books were on top of the case, an end one lying flat, with several others leaning against it and the remaining few standing. It looked as though the bookends had been removed and the books allowed to fall any which way.

"What kind of bookends?"

"Quite unusual. She bought them at an antique shop—I was with her. Big, black, shaped like frogs . . . very heavy."

"What were they made of?"

"They felt like lead, but actually they were pottery . . . something called Rockwood. Arts and crafts."

"What do you suppose happened to them?"

"I have no idea. Maybe she got tired of them—I haven't been here for a while."

Everything else was so orderly, it seemed unlike the Faith I was getting to know to leave books in a jumble.

I glanced at some of the titles, on the top and on the shelves. They looked mostly like textbooks: *Guide to English Literature, Principles of Organic Chemistry,* things like that. Also there were a few classic novels: *The Age of Innocence, The Scarlet Letter,* Jane Austen, which also may have dated back to school years. Some old children's books completed the assortment. Apparently Faith didn't try to keep up with modern literature—at least not to the extent of patronizing a bookstore.

I asked Fumi, "Was Faith one-track? Did she care about anything except science?"

"Oh, she cared about other things. We went to concerts and

movies sometimes. We went shopping, took walks. But l guess you could say it was all secondary. She was dedicated."

We moved on to the bedroom. Bedstead, dark wood. Matching dresser and dressing table with a triptych of mirrors. A white embroidered runner holding a bottle of cologne and an ornate sterling silver hairbrush, comb and mirror in art nouveau design. It looked like stuff Faith had grown up with.

"If she went away," I said, "she didn't take her brush and comb."

"She might not have wanted these," said Fumi. "Plastics are better for travel. Lighter."

On two of the walls were a pair of routine nineteenth century prints, English countryside—reproductions, the sort you might find in a hotel. On a third wall was the same group photo Wells had showed me, the lab crew at the swimming pool. Evidently this held some importance for Faith. Then, on the bureau, framed, was an enlargement of a snapshot: a man and woman, their dress indicating that it had been taken some years ago. They had posed on the front steps of a shingled house on what must have been a cold day; he in an overcoat, she a cloth coat with a fur collar. Both wore hats and she had gloves on. Solid citizens.

"Her parents?" I asked.

"Yes. I've never met them."

"Where do they live?"

"Idaho—Pocatello."

"Could she have gone out to be with them?"

"It's possible. But they didn't see each other very often, and I don't know why just now, without saying anything to anybody . . ."

"If the showdown didn't go the way she wanted . . . maybe for moral support . . ."

"Maybe, but somehow I don't have the feeling that's where she'd get it."

When we both were satisfied we'd seen all we had to, Arco trailed us out, locking the door. As we went down in the elevator, I said, "One more thing, Mr. Arco. It'd be a big help if you could introduce me to Dr. Frawley's neighbors—the ones on either side and just below. They might have heard something, and those on the same floor might have talked to her. Do they all go to work, do you know?"

"Yes." He sounded bored with being cooperative.

"Then pretty soon they might be coming home?"

We had reached the ground floor and Arco stood back to let us precede him out, but he didn't answer my question.

"I'll be glad to pay you for your trouble," I added.

This had the desired effect. He said, "Be here . . . twenty minutes," and went off down the hall.

Out on the sidewalk I told Fumi, "There's no point in your sticking around. I'll walk you back to the tram, then I'll just be in time for Arco."

She glanced at her watch. "I can stay longer."

"Not necessary, but thanks. I'll keep you informed."

The water, to our right as we retraced our steps, sparkled under the westering sun. A tugboat towed a barge up river. Skyward a gondola was sailing from the big island to the little.

"What do you think?" I asked.

"I don't like the way it looks."

"Neither do I."

I had a few minutes wait for Arco, then another few before the first of the immediate neighbors walked into the lobby. She was an overweight, perspiring middleaged woman with a discontented mouth. She carried a D'Agostino's plastic shopping bag.

"Mrs. Crocker—" Arco spoke to her. "Ask you something: You here over weekend?"

"This last weekend? No, we were out of town. Why?"

"You here, was gonna ask you a question . . ."

The elevator door opened. Mrs. Crocker stepped in.

That took care of the neighbor who lived to one side of Frawley.

Maria Marinello, the tenant on the other, arrived home fifteen minutes later. She was tall, tanned, handsome, with a dancer's body and ash-blond hair tied in a pony tail. Arco gave me the opening to introduce myself. When I explained what I was trying to find out, she replied, "Yes, I did hear something. If you want to come up I can tell you about it."

Marinello's apartment—the living room at least—was barer

than Faith's. She was indeed a dancer: a ballet bar, portable, about five feet long, stood against one wall. Simple, clean-lined furniture also was ranged along the walls, leaving the central space free, presumably for exercise and practice. Took me back to the days with Doreen and her perennial complaint that our living quarters were too cramped for this kind of setup.

Two Siamese cats had been waiting at the door when it was opened, and after twining through their mistress's legs went bounding off together, over sofa and chairs, tangling and spatting.

As she turned on the air conditioner, Marinello asked, "Lemonade?"

"Thanks, that'd be great."

"Saturday night," she began when we were seated across from each other, cool glasses in hand. "Must have been around eight o'clock—I was getting ready to go out. My bedroom's up against her living room. There was an argument."

"Could you hear what it was about?"

"Not very well. Usually it's quiet from her side. I'd never heard voices raised like that before."

"Was one of them a man's?"

"Oh, yes."

"And the other was hers?"

"It sounded like her."

"Did you make out any of what they were saying?"

"Some—but they were moving around and not all of it was clear. At one point he yelled, 'If you'll stop being hysterical for a minute!' Then a little later she said something I couldn't make much sense out of. Not that I was trying very hard . . . it bothers me when people fight."

"What was it—can you remember?"

"Yes, because it was so odd. About his uncle—Uncle Gene."

"What about him?"

"'I'll make damn sure everybody knows about your fucking Uncle Gene's—' Like that. She was really mad."

"Your fucking Uncle Gene's what?"

"I didn't catch the rest of it."

"What else did they fight about?"

"That's all I can tell you. After that I escaped."

"And at that point was it quiet?"

"Quiet as the grave."

Two men shared the apartment directly under Faith's. One was home by the time I'd finished with Marinello: Guy Brammell. Arco took me to his door and after he introduced me I handed him ten bucks and excused him.

"Please forgive the informal attire," Brammell said as he waved me in. In his late sixties or early seventies, he wore black cotton harem pants with a white cable-knit top. His feet were gold-slippered.

Much attention had been paid here to decor. Luxurious upholstery fabrics. Brass and tole lamps. Draperies with swags. Tinsel pictures of actors hamming up Shakespeare. A splendid oriental rug.

I complimented him on the furnishings; they obviously meant a lot to him. He seemed pleased. "Would you care for some iced tea? Or possibly something stronger?"

Something stronger would have been welcome after the recent lemonade upstairs, but tea seemed to be his preference. I'd learned that in trying to pump people for information one usually got farthest by playing to their tastes, so I said thank you, tea would be fine.

"I'll be just a sec. Make yourself comfortable."

While he was off in the kitchen, I inspected the dozen or so photographs on one wall. They were of show-biz celebrities and all were affectionately inscribed to Guy. I gathered from the effusions that he had done their hair and thereby made them stars.

When he returned carrying a tray with two tall glasses, a pitcher and a plate of cookies, we settled on a sofa with a coffee table before us and he poured. The tea, I had to admit, was delicious.

"That's quite an impressive picture gallery," I remarked. "And every one of them loves you."

"Yes, I think I can honestly say they do."

"Let me explain more fully why I'm here," I said. Arco, I gathered, had given him a rough idea. Just then the door opened and a younger man walked in. He was very good looking. I rose.

"Jack," Brammell said, "this is Mr. Swain. He's here about one of our neighbors."

Jack was wearing a beautifully tailored lightweight suit that set off his broad shoulders and narrow waist.

"Who's that?"

"Her name is Dr. Frawley—Faith Frawley."

"I don't think I know her."

"I didn't think I did either, but we've spoken in the elevator. Fetch yourself a glass and have some of this iced tea."

"Be right with you."

We waited till he was back. He had removed his jacket and loosened his tie.

"Faith Frawley is the lady who lives above us," Brammell informed him. "Rather plain but pleasant. You've said hello."

"Yes, now I know." He picked up the pitcher and poured.

"Mr. Swain wants to ask us something about her."

"I doubt there's much we can tell since we didn't even know who she is. But do ask."

"Dr. Frawley does research in medical science and she works at the Krinsky Research Center. So do I. I'm trying to find out what happened to her."

"She's what—disappeared?"

"Seems to have. She didn't show up for work yesterday, or today. Didn't tell anyone she wasn't going to."

"I see," said Jack. "Are you sure it wasn't voluntary?"

"No, but that wouldn't be her style. She's very conscientious—she would have given advance notice. I came over to check with the neighbors—whether she might have said something to someone, or if they heard anything."

"And?" said Brammell.

"Saturday night a woman upstairs—lives to her right—heard an argument through the wall. A fight really. Also unusual; first time there's ever been any disturbance."

"Well, we heard something too," said Jack. "Guy, remember?"

"Yes, like drilling."

"Power tool of some sort."

"What time would this have been?"

"About ten," said Brammell. "We'd rented *Swann in Love* and just started it on the VCR."

29

"It was very annoying," said Jack.

"How long did it go on?"

"The disturbance?" Brammell pursed his lips. "Too long. About half an hour."

"I think it was less than that, but it was damned intrusive!"

"We turned off the VCR till it stopped."

"Are you sure," I asked, "it came from Dr. Frawley's apartment?"

"Oh, absolutely," said Brammell.

"Had you ever heard anything like that from up there before?"

They looked at each other. "I'd say no, wouldn't you, Jack?"

"I don't remember ever," Jack agreed.

"Dr. Frawley and I had little conversations in the elevator," Brammell said. "Once we compared dates when we moved in and she'd been here before we were. So we didn't even hear any sounds of her getting settled."

I thanked them for their help.

"Do have a cookie before you go," said Brammell.

I took one, a lacy chocolate confection. It melted on the tongue.

"Bloomie's," sighed Brammell rapturously. "Pure heaven having it one jump away!"

I stood, removed a card from my wallet and handed it to him. Together they walked me to the door. They promised that if they remembered anything that might be relevant, or if some other neighbor said something, they'd let me know.

The sun was hanging somewhere beyond Bloomingdale's when I emerged onto Main Street. I reviewed what I had learned or noticed during my short stay on Roosevelt Island:

Two black frog bookends had vanished from Faith's apartment.

She didn't drink but she had one bottle on hand, perhaps for a regular caller, and the label was not one you saw every day.

On Saturday night fellow tenants had heard loud sounds—some of them angry—from her normally quiet apartment.

The male party to the fight apparently had an uncle named Gene and Faith was threatening to expose him.

I had no idea how these pieces fitted together or whether they even did.

THREE

The first thing I did when I walked into my office next morning was ask Altagracia to call all the hospitals and see whether Faith, or a likely candidate among amnesia victims, had been admitted. If not, she was to try the morgue.

Half an hour later Colombia's loss, my gain, reported no success—if that was the word. I decided I'd better have another chat with Wells.

I found him in his office, editing a manuscript. He pushed it aside, set his pen down on the desk.

"How did it go on the island?"

"I don't know. The little we found out doesn't seem to get us anywhere."

"We?"

"Dr. Tashamira went with me to check out the apartment. Then I interviewed a couple of neighbors. Three actually. They heard a disturbance—some sort of a fight—but they didn't make much sense out of it."

Wells looked puzzled. "A fight . . . at Faith's?"

"Yes."

"She's not a fighting woman. When was it?"

"Saturday night."

"That's very strange." He leaned forward over the desk, propped himself on his elbows. "Did anybody catch anything . . . any of the words?"

"Something about somebody's uncle. . . ."

"Faith's?"

"No, the other person's."

"The other one's a man?"

"That's right.

"So what about his uncle?"

31

"They didn't hear enough to make anything out of it."

He shook his head. "Well, that's not much help."

I moved on to a new subject. "I'm wondering if it mightn't be a good idea to interview everybody in your lab. Faith might have said something to somebody, or they might have noticed something. Do I have your permission?"

"Sure thing. I just can't imagine what this uncle business . . ." He straightened up and called out, "Sally!"

His secretary poked her head in. "Sally, will you round up the gang—get everybody into the conference room . . . say, ten minutes from now?"

He turned again to me. "This way you can tell 'em all at once what you're doing, then schedule individual appointments. The conference room will be yours until you're finished."

"Thanks. I've brought my tape recorder. If we have to call in the police later, they can listen to this stuff if they want—not have to ask the same questions all over again."

With ten minutes to kill, Wells returned to the neighbors' reports, going over the same ground we'd just covered, as though the second time around might yield up something more comprehensible.

I had a sudden thought.

"What if it wasn't Faith?"

"You mean someone else in her apartment?"

"She might have given someone her key . . . or someone might have got hold of it. . . ."

"I guess anything's possible." He frowned. "In science, of course, the rule is always to favor the simplest explanation."

I knew the rule of parsimony, as it was called. But what was the simplest explanation here? That Faith was so angry she'd sounded off uncharacteristically—or that persons unknown had somehow got access to her apartment and were using it as a battleground? If the latter, then presumably it had something to do with her, since she was now missing. But that began to be pretty complicated. Clearly, the simplest explanation—the one to go with—was that Faith had lost her temper and self-control.

I realized there was more to tell and moved on to Brammell and Jack and the power tool that had interrupted *Swann in*

Love. In conclusion I mentioned Altagracia's check of hospitals and the morgue.

"Not quite the job you thought you were taking on here, is it?" grimaced Wells.

"Hardly."

"Well, I hope this is all cleared up soon. How are you adjusting to life in New York?"

I told him I'd lived here before and felt out of things when I didn't.

"Maybe some time soon you'll come up to Bedford Hills and spend the day. Bring a friend."

"I'd like to." At the moment I wouldn't have known whom to invite. Hazel had rented a summer place on one of the Thimble Islands off Connecticut with a college chum. I hadn't yet met a woman here who interested me. Except, of course . . . but why torment myself?

Sally returned to announce that the whole crew, with the exception of a technician sent out for coffee and croissants, was waiting for us across the hall.

They were seated at the long conference table, carrying on conversations that stopped when we entered. There were about a dozen in all, including Ms. (or was it Dr.?) Martin, Fumi, Barnard and several others I recognized. One was an Indian woman—from India—with a diamond in the side of her nose. Two were dark-skinned men. I wasn't sure about the Indian's age, but everyone else was on Beth Martin's side of the generation gap.

I remained standing with Wells as he introduced me (a reintroduction to some) and explained that I was trying to find out why Faith hadn't showed up for the last three days. He interrupted himself to ask, "Have any of you by any chance heard from her?" No one had. "Well, before we scare the daylights out of Faith's family and bring in the police, we want to explore every possible lead on our own. Bert's going to ask each of you some questions, and it may be that some remark of Faith's, or something you've heard or seen—even if it didn't seem significant at the time—could provide a clue. One caution: please don't say anything about any of this outside the lab. Publicity at this point won't help, and it might hurt."

33

"Now that you know why we're all here," I said, "I'd like to set up a schedule. I shouldn't need more than a few minutes with each of you." I looked at my watch. "It's now ten-fifteen. Who would be free this morning?"

About half raised their hands. From among them I chose—naturally—to start with Martin. The others were given appointments and let go. I moved down the table to where she was sitting and took the adjoining chair.

Switching on the recorder, I asked, "You're *Dr.* Martin?"

"Not yet."

"But you're planning a career in the biological sciences?"

"If I'm good enough."

I could now get a real look at her: blue eyes with surprising dark lashes, straight blond hair to the shoulders and the best soap-and-water complexion. The crisp white lab coat suggested a purity of person and purpose. I was letting myself get carried away and knew it. I was enjoying it.

"How well do you know Dr. Frawley?"

"Not very. We say hello. She's in B, I'm in A."

"The two rooms in the lab?"

"That's right."

"Did you hear her say anything about weekend plans—for this last weekend?"

"No. But then I wouldn't have been likely to."

"Have you sensed anything unusual about her lately?" I answered for her: "No, you're in A, she's in B."

That got a smile.

"Has anyone else said anything about her?"

She shook her head, the curtain of hair swinging slightly. "I wish I could help."

Human will power is a wonderful thing . . . infinitely flexible, at least in my case. In the little time we'd been talking, my determination to leave Beth strictly alone had softened to the point of collapse. After all, there was no reason why an older man and a younger woman couldn't be friends. We didn't have to end up in bed—unless she wanted to. There *are* girls who go for older men. Probably something to do with their feelings about their fathers, but that didn't necessarily mean it was wrong. Maybe she'd let me take her to a movie some time . . . or dinner.

I asked her: "Would you consider having dinner some time? It would give me great pleasure."

She colored, hesitated. I could see her thinking. Then: "Yes. That would be nice."

"When would be convenient?"

"I can't this week. How about next?"

I was off and running. "Monday?"

"Let's say Tuesday?"

If there was something else I should be asking now, something about—what was her name? Faith Frawley—I wasn't able to think of it.

By two o'clock I'd had a chance to tape everybody including the technician who'd been out when we started—a young man growing a beard, apparently itchy—and had come up with exactly nothing.

Again with Wells's assistance I set myself a further task. On his say-so, Krinsky's personnel office made the dossiers of every individual in his lab available to me, and beginning at three o'clock and resuming the next morning I slogged through them all. My thinking was that maybe Faith's path and that of someone else working under Wells might have crossed in the past—on a campus or through some cooperative study, possibly being conducted at different institutions. Maybe an old score, or rivalry, had been settled over the weekend.

The dossiers told me a lot about people's backgrounds. Beth came from Cleveland, model student, no surprises. By eleven a.m. when I'd read the last I'd found no hint of any previous links.

After lunch I was back in Wells's office.

"What do you suggest now?" he asked.

"I'm afraid we don't have any choice at this point—we're going to have to notify Faith's parents."

"They'll be terribly upset."

"The first thing they'll want to know is what the police are doing."

"Yes, of course." A sigh. "I'll let you deal with the police if you don't mind. I'll phone the Frawleys."

Faith had gone far in her career—though perhaps not far

enough to satisfy her—for someone from a small western city. Was hers the all-too-familiar story of the starry-eyed girl who'd been drawn to New York by a dream, to end up defeated or dead? A minute's reflection told me that Faith hardly sounded starry eyed and might not even have chosen to be in New York. It was probably just that New York was where she had a chance to do her kind of work.

As for the ending, I wasn't yet ready to concede the worst.

I had a connection at One Police Plaza from my *Record* days, Albert Battaglia. A former homicide detective, he now held an administrative job. I took the subway down to see him.

He'd lost weight and color but I told him he looked great. He told me the same thing. At least I knew I still had a trace of my Florida tan.

"What can I do for you?" he said, popping a pill.

"A woman in one of our labs has dropped out of sight."

"When?"

"She didn't come in on Monday. Last seen Friday afternoon."

"Is this your first contact with the police about it?"

"Yes. I've been doing some checking on my own. You may remember Krinsky had some negative publicity before I got there: head of the purchasing department was lining his own pockets. I was asked to keep Faith Frawley's name out of the news as long as I could. I haven't been able to come up with anything, so now we have to notify her parents out west that she's missing and we feel you guys have got to be in on it— but we'd sure as hell like to avoid more bad press."

"Maybe you should've got us guys in on it in the first place."

"Yeah, maybe we should, but I've done some of your groundwork." I told him about the taped interviews.

When he heard where Faith lived, he said the case fell into the jurisdiction of the 114th Precinct in Queens—across the river from Roosevelt Island on the opposite side from Manhattan. He picked up the phone and got a Detective Lynch on the line.

"Al Battaglia. Friend here with me, handles public relations for the Krinsky Research Center. Place in Manhattan, works on cancer, things like that. . . . Okay, you know about it. His name's Swain. Bert Swain . . . good man, used to write for the old *Record*. The situation is this." After making the same pitch I had for no publicity, he repeated the facts.

Ringing off, Al informed me, "One you want to talk to is Lieutenant Balch. He'll handle it as a missing person. Try him in an hour or so—he's out now." He noted the name and number on a memo pad, tore off the sheet and handed it to me. "Tell him Kevin Lynch referred you. Call me some day and let's have lunch."

"You're on." Some day maybe I will. Promising to have lunch in New York is like saying bless you after somebody sneezes.

The Frawleys lost no time catching a plane and were in town early the next afternoon, Friday. I met them in Wells's office. They were recognizable from the photo in Faith's bedroom. They looked old in a deteriorated way. I wondered how much of their aging had occurred overnight following Wells's call.

Lieutenant Balch, when I'd phoned him yesterday, had promised to have someone on the case today; thus Wells and I could assure the couple that the police were actively involved. Balch sounded like a nice guy; he'd said "Sure" when I proposed that we keep in touch and share information. We had arranged that I'd bring the Frawleys to see him.

Before we left Krinsky for our meeting with Balch, I gathered up the interview tapes. The three of us then took a taxi to the East Side and over the Fifty-ninth Street bridge to Queens. Crossing the bridge, Mrs. Frawley, at the window, looked down on Roosevelt Island and remarked bitterly, "You would have thought she might have been safe *there* at least."

Frawley said, "She wouldn't listen to us. Had to come to New York."

I gathered they had visited their daughter a few years ago and had feared and hated the big city. Making conversation with them wasn't easy, but I learned that Mr. Frawley was in feed and grain and Mrs. was what used to be called a housewife, today's homemaker. Faith's refusal to stay put in "Pocatella", marry, bear children and be her parents' joy and comfort in their declining years was a form of willfulness that strained their understanding. But there was no doubting the genuineness of their present pain.

Balch was large and rumpled. He thanked me for the tapes and asked if anyone minded if he smoked. Whatever their usual position on smoking, the Frawleys couldn't care less at the moment; their total concern was Faith. Of course there was nothing he could tell them.

"We're just getting started," he said. "We had a team at your daughter's apartment this morning, checking things out. Mr Swain here has done some unofficial investigating, but missing persons has to allow a reasonable time for an individual to turn up before we call on our full resources.—Unless of course it's a child or someone with a medical or mental condition. Hundreds of people drop out of sight in our city every day, and a surprising number of them resurface. Maybe out of town, or out of the country. There are a thousand reasons why they disappear. Sometimes the folks we're closest to surprise us. It could be amnesia. Mr. Swain has checked all the hospitals; we'll check them again."

"How about the morgue?" Frawley asked in a constricted voice.

"I did that too," I said.

Balch went on, "We'll do the same with homeless shelters, bus depots, train stations and subways. If your daughter's disoriented she could be sitting in a subway car right now. The word's out to the transit police."

He shifted his soft bulk in his chair and ground out the barely-smoked cigarette in an ashtray. Without thinking, he lit another. I guessed he was trying to stop smoking and unconsciously figured he was getting there if he didn't finish any one cigarette.

"I promise you, Mr. and Mrs. Frawley," he said, "now that we're on it we'll give it everything we've got—and we'll keep you posted . . . anything we find out we'll tell you—at once."

"We're planning to stay on here," said Frawley, "until you do find something out."

Balch released a contrail through his nostrils. "That's up to you of course, but unless you have other business in these parts I wouldn't recommend it. It can be quite a while and the frustration's that much worse if you're in a strange place just waiting. I gather you got here pretty fast this time—you can always hop another plane."

The Frawleys exchanged bleak glances; I could see that leaving would mean acknowledging a certain powerlessness.

"You still have the subways and shelters, all those places, to check," Frawley said. "I don't think we ought to go until you've had a chance to do that."

"At least another night, Roy," his wife concurred.

They had informed Wells and me that they would want to go to Faith's apartment, so I brought this up. I'd be accompanying them. Would we have any trouble getting in?

"I'll see that you don't," said Balch. "There's a police detail on the island; I'll alert them."

We all rose and the Frawleys summoned up thank-yous.

In a taxi on the way to the island from the Queens side, Mrs. Frawley said, "I guess we'll just have to pray to the Lord."

We were dropped in front of Faith's house. Clearly, word from Balch had preceded us: Arco, the super, was in the lobby when we arrived and had the keys ready. He entered the apartment with us, and he and I remained near the front door together while the parents wandered slowly through. They gazed searchingly at the living room and its contents, then advanced to the bedroom. Wordless. I visualized them standing before the photos of themselves and Faith in her group. I wondered if, studying their own picture, they saw how they had aged.

They came out of the bedroom looking depleted.

As Arco locked the door behind us, Frawley said to him, "I want to pay next month's rent. Where do I do that?"

"Managemen' office. I show you."

I went with them and stood by while Frawley, standing at the counter, bent over, hand shaking, wrote out a check.

The three of us returned to Manhattan by the tram. At the bottom of the stairs we said goodbye. They thanked me for my help, I reiterated Balch's promise to let them know anything we learned the minute we learned it.

FOUR

With the NYPD on the case, I took a breather from Faith Frawley. Beth Martin had given me her phone number. Monday evening I used it to set up Tuesday's date.

She sounded pleased to hear from me.

"Are we still on for dinner tomorrow?"

"I'm looking forward to it."

"Shall I pick you up at seven?"

"Fine. We could start with a drink here."

That was real friendly. "Be happy to. Any kind of food you specially like—or dislike?"

"Japanese . . . I'm not fond of that. Anything else."

"Good. See you then."

When I put the phone down, I hugged myself. Maybe forty-seven didn't look so old to her after all. I hadn't told her my age; probably she thought I was younger. Or she could have seen me as interestingly mature.

That's what I was, actually. Newspaper man . . . been around, brushed shoulders with all kinds of people. Experienced joy . . . sorrow. Fatherhood.

I peered into the mirror over the sofa, looking for signs of interesting maturity. What gazed back was the familiar face, a little the worse for wear. But maybe there was something appealing to a young woman in its character creases and furrows.

I sat down on the sofa and daydreamed. If things got cosy between us and I started getting physical, would it shock Beth and spoil everything?

A dilemma. I didn't want to hold back if there was a chance that ours could be one of those April-September relationships, filling a niche for each of us on our separate tracks in time, enriching us both. It could be transient, yet leave an afterglow. Beth would find a man closer to her own age for the long haul, I'd eventually settle down, I expected, with an older woman. But for now . . .

Whoa, boy! Don't get ahead of yourself. Tomorrow's just dinner. Let's take it easy and see what happens.

What happened was that Beth, even prettier than I remembered, opened the door and invited me in. She was wearing a light lemony jacket over a short white dress. As I entered, a woman rose from where she was sitting and smiled at me.

"My mother's visiting from Cleveland."

Mom came forward. "Good evening." She appeared to be a well-kept late forties, quite smartly turned out in a black-and-white print set off by jet jewelry. Her hair was a shade darker than Beth's and considerably shorter. She sported glasses with bits of sparkle in the frames.

"Hello, how are you? Mrs. Martin, is it?"

She held out her hand."Right. Married to the same husband for twenty-eight years."

"Dad died two years ago," said Beth. "What would you like to drink?"

I was pretty sure she wouldn't have my first choice, so I said, "Bourbon, if you have it—or Scotch—any kind of whiskey."

"Mom drinks bourbon, too." As she crossed the room I saw there were several bottles—one of them a Coke—on a dropleaf table, with three glasses, awaiting my arrival.

"Why don't you sit here?" suggested Mom, indicating an overstuffed chair—her seat until I walked in.

"I don't want to take your—"

"No, no. It's a man's chair—you should be comfortable." She waved me down into it. "Beth tells me you work where she does?"

"Same building, different departments. I write about things, Beth does them."

"She was always a good student. Wanted to be a scientist from when she was a little girl."

I was beginning to feel slightly uncomfortable. Beth was still a child compared to Mrs. Martin and me. I had designs on this child. They would not be realized—at least not in the present location—with Mrs. Martin around. It was a relief when Beth handed me my glass and I had something to hold onto and make business with. When Mrs. Martin was given hers a minute later and Beth poured for herself from the Coke bottle, I raised my drink to Mom: "Here's to a pleasant stay." And after we'd all taken a swallow: "Do you get to New York often?"

"Not as often as I'd like. I don't know anyone here."

"At home Mom has a lot of friends. She's the president of her bridge club."

"That's nice."

We went on eking out conversation. Finally, when I felt courtesy had been served, I looked at my watch and said, "Well, shall we take off? I've reserved for quarter to eight."

Both women stood up. I put my glass aside and did likewise.

"You won't mind if my mother comes along?"

"I promise to behave myself . . only speak when spoken to."

Something started happening in my eyes: suddenly there was a band in front of them, dark, bloody, blocking vision. . . . I was seeing red.

"The reservation was for two!" I said, barely controlling my voice. "If you and your mother want to keep it—La Plage on West Sixteenth Street! Tell 'em I sent you!"

I left them standing.

Down on the sidewalk I came to a stop. I had no idea where I was heading and my sight wasn't too hot. Telling myself my reaction was excessive, I made an effort to calm down. Beth's chutzpah was bigger than mine; she had showed me up for the old fool I was—I ought to thank her for it.

And here I'd been worrying that *I* might be taking advantage of a naive young thing.

The positive side, if there was one, was that she couldn't have found me too repulsive or she wouldn't have tried to fob me off on Mom.

It is to laugh, and die a little.

At the moment I was in no shape to laugh.

Beth lived in an ungentrified neighborhood just off lower Second Avenue. Not a part of town I was particularly familiar with, but I knew a watering hole when I saw one—and Shar-

42

key's, a short walk up Second, had a tawdry neon-ed front that appealed to me in my down-and-dirty mood. It looked like the perfect contrast to the restaurant that'd just been reviewed in the *Times*—where I'd expected to dine. I pushed past a young couple hesitating whether to go in and found myself in a smoky room with a long bar. A TV over the bar was tuned to the baseball game that plays endlessly in saloons until it's replaced by the nonstop football game. It was a little early for a crowd but there were enough bodies to make a lot of good noise. Leaning over a vacant stool I placed my order for Irish; if I sat down I'd be asking for asphyxiation by smoke from both sides.

When the drink came, I moved back from the bar and surveyed the people lined up at it. A fellatio-lipped brunette seated where it curved at the end looked back at me with a direct, challenging gaze. I engaged her eyes to test how long she could hold it. When we ended in a draw, I started moving toward her; one of the stools next to her was unoccupied.

"Saving this for me?" I was already pulling it back.

"Could be."

She was another smoker, I saw, but if she gave me lung cancer it would be in a good cause.

Her highball glass was almost empty. "What are you drinking?"

"Dewar's."

"Scotland meet Ireland." I touched my glass to hers, then raised it to catch the bartender's attention. "Another Dewar's for the lady."

"You Irish?" she said.

"Not particularly."

"I haven't seen you here before."

"My first time. Name's Bert Swain."

"Mine's Randi . . . spelled with an i."

"Hello, Randi." I wanted to say "Don't care how it's spelled as long as you live up to it," but after Beth I had some way to go before getting back a hundred percent self-confidence.

"What do you do, Bert?"

"You mean for a living?"

She nodded.

"I work for the Krinsky Research Center. Heard of it?"

"Sure. You one of these guys in a white smock?"

"Just a business suit. I'm press relations—tell the world what the white smocks are up to."

"Sounds interesting."

"Sometimes. What's your line?"

"Travel agency—office manager."

"You get cut rates when you take trips?"

"Sometimes."

"You sound like a person to know."

"That depends." Her drink was set down before her. As she picked it up she said, "I don't usually hang out like this by myself."

"I don't either. I just got stood up. No, that isn't it—I stood *her* up."

"Why?"

"Dinner date—first time—and when I ring the bell here's her old lady in from Cleveland and wouldn't it be just too ducky-peachy to bring her along?"

Randi laughed. "What did you do?"

"Here I am—alone."

"Not where you were planning to end up."

"This just happens to be the first bar I see and I am in need of a drink. What's your excuse?"

"Fight with my boyfriend. He was sitting where you're sitting. Now my ex-boyfriend."

"That serious?"

"Not our first fight but definitely the last."

"Sorry."

"Don't be."

"Sounds like we were fated to meet tonight."

Fated or not, we took advantage of our situation. After a second drink for me, we moved on to a Chinese noodle shop around the corner. By then, the blood had cleared from my eyes and I was able to put away some food.

There wasn't any question of what came next. Her place being closer, we ended up there . . . a walkup, back apartment on the second floor. It was furnished in neo-Victorian: tasseled draperies, converted oil lamps, harem cushions and gewgaws—too much stuff for a couple of small rooms. Out of character, too, with the chrome-plated front she presented. And certainly an incongruous background for the dialogue we had before stripping and falling into bed—her condoms or mine. I was equipped with the plain old-fashioned kind; she had them ribbed, for added sensation. Back in Florida my women and I had been going at it long enough to not to worry about safe. New York was something else. I put on a ribbed.

I was still feeling enough anger against Beth so that I fell to with brutal fierceness. She seemed to like it; her moans were as much from pain as pleasure, but she didn't try to make me go easy. I heard my own full-throttle moans. (Usually I was the quiet type.) The ribbed condom was an unqualified success—though the real cause of tonight's kick was revenge: not only against Beth but against women in general for a lot of frustrations I'd suffered.

We exhausted ourselves with a couple of repeat performances and slept later next morning than either of us expected. It had been my plan to go home first thing and change clothes, but it was too late for that, there was barely time for a shower and coffee. Randi looked pretty good even before replacing last night's makeup with today's, and she tactfully avoided any lingering glances at me till I'd shaved with the ex-boyfriend's razor and bathed. I thought I'd like to see her again and hoped she felt the same. I brought out a business card.

"If you'd like a return engagement . . ."

"Why not?"

"Here, let me write my home phone so you could get me after work." I uncapped my pen.

We were in the mini-kitchen; she tore a scrap off a shopping-list pad and wrote out her phone numbers, here and at the travel agency.

Then we walked out together, into the sultry sunshine.

Before I knew what was happening I was assaulted—grabbed by the shoulder, swung around and punched in the face.

"Clyde! Let go! Let him go, you sonofabitch!" Randi was trying to pull Clyde off; he was hanging on. I flailed out, hit his arm—pushed. He fell back a step—a wiry, blazing-eyed, nasty-looking customer in walking shorts and T-shirt, a gold chain around his neck. As he came at me again, I reached for the chain, giving it such a yank that it broke. I threw it into the street—as far as I could. This diverted his attention from me as, fouling the air with bad language, he scrambled after it. Randi took the opportunity to seize the door handle of a cab that had been waiting for the light to change—which, thank God, it now did.

"Get in! Hurry!"

I needed no urging. Before Clyde could get back to us we were gone. I suddenly realized that my right cheekbone hurt. Seeing me touch it, Randi put up her own hand to caress it. Though the pressure was gentle, I winced.

"Poor baby."

"If that was your boyfriend," I said, "he doesn't seem to think he's ex."

"I'm terribly sorry. I had no idea he'd do anything like this. I wonder if he saw us last night or whether he just decided to wait outside this morning and see if I came out with somebody."

"I didn't have a chance to put up a fight—didn't even know he was there."

"Of course not. Sneak attack—I'll never forgive him!"

Even if I *had* known, there was no guarantee I'd have done any better. I'd never been good with my fists. As a kid I avoided fights instead of trying to learn how to box. It wasn't so much a fear of getting hurt as of looking ridiculous through ineptitude.

I wasn't a kid any more and I'd looked ridiculous more than once and it hadn't killed me. But not being able to defend myself, especially in New York City, could kill. I wasn't going to be put off seeing Randi again, and Clyde wasn't ready to give her up.

It was time to take boxing lessons.

FIVE

Michael, the owner and my instructor at Midtown Boxing Gym, wasn't too impressed by the reason I gave for taking up the sport. He didn't say so, but I think he would have liked to tell me "If you want to defend yourself on the street, go learn karate." According to the little lecture with which he prefaced my first lesson, "Boxing is psychology . . . strategy. Boxers are always looking for weaknesses. You study the other guy, see what part of the body he's trying to protect. That's where he feels vulnerable. Then you hit hard somewhere else, and when he tries to cover that place you let him have it where he's weakest."

Under sudden attack in the street I'd hardly have time to study the other guy. Karate probably would have made more sense. But I stayed with Michael because I liked him.

He could see I wasn't going to turn into a real fighter, so building me up with exercises and exhortations bored him. Because he knew I worked with words on my job and he loved language, he used our sessions as opportunities for verbal self-expression. I put up with it because what he said interested me and while he was talking he'd lose count of how many times I pulled the handles that lifted weights or forget whether I'd done enough pedal pumping or hefting of barbells. I was only shortchanging myself of course, but I rationalized that I was making up for it by going at the punching bag hot and heavy and skipping rope enthusiastically. Michael was from Panama, with a south-of-the-border complexion, tall without an extra ounce of flesh on him. His English, though accented, was excellent. He was used to my type of dilettante; there were several others among the businessmen who came to the gym when I did, between seven-thirty and eight in the morning. We were known as white collar boxers. The pros, actual or would-be, worked out in the afternoon. A couple of the fellows in my group were serious and good. It was a pleasure to watch them spar, either with one another or paid sparring partners. After a few sessions I acquired a sparring partner, a gentle black man named Ferdie. He fended off my blows almost languidly and never hit me too hard.

Michael would often greet me with "Well, did you have a drink yesterday?" In his book you couldn't drink and box. And because I wanted to please him I went through some days without whiskey, wine or beer. Then I felt virtuous. Other times, tempted, I said what the hell and broke training—such as it was. I would have liked to be one of the serious ones. Gradually the idea that I was going to be able to demolish jealous boyfriends, muggers and murderers with my pugilistic skill receded, replaced by simple pleasure in doing some kind of exercise in agreeable surroundings.

Back at Westside Medical Center there were still problems to be dealt with.

A second eminent researcher, Bernard Tallman, followed the example set by Philip Etcheverry and left Krinsky for employment elsewhere—in this instance Johns Hopkins. As with Etcheverry, I succeeded in persuading Tallman not to air his gripe against "Darryl" Cromart, and since his colleagues neither signed another petition nor rose in revolt, his departure created no public stir.

Hazel asked me to escort her to what threatened to be a stormy meeting. It had been called by opponents of the expansion program, and Hazel was one of those defending the medical center's position. She said she needed me for moral support.

We arrived at the local high school auditorium a few minutes before eight to find an overflow crowd. Hostility was in the air. People were clustered in the aisles or standing in front of their seats talking from row to row. Voices were strident, eyes hard. Hazel was supposed to occupy one of the chairs on the stage, but since no one else was up there we stood against the wall toward the rear waiting for somebody to take charge. I didn't like the idea of Hazel having to confront this mob. Neither did she. She reached for my hand and we gave each other a squeeze.

At eight-ten a statuesque woman came on from the wings and stepped up to the miked lectern. It took a few moments for the place to settle down. Then she loosed a throaty contralto: "Good evening, ladies and gentlemen . . . neighbors. I'm Rosalyn McInerney, chair of COMCE, Committee in Opposition to Medical Center Expansion. This meeting has been called to solidify our stand against the building program that would cut off the light and views of many of us here and cost us all more traffic, noise and pollution. After numerous attempts to bring representatives of the medical center and its hired fund raisers to an open forum ["That's a lie!" whispered Hazel], we have at last extracted a promise of their participation tonight.

"Where," she asked, peering out skeptically into the audience, "where might these . . . spokespersons . . . be?" Picking "spokespersons" up with a pair of tongs and holding it as far from her nose as possible.

"I'm here," said Hazel, and started toward the front. Two men rose where they'd been seated and moved forward. Dr. T. Graydon Stokes, director of the hospital and Hazel's boss, was known to me by sight, and I'd met the professional campaign manager from a fund-raising company, Ben Podesta. There were four chairs waiting, three in a group, one off to the side. The trio took seats together, looking like so many sacrificial victims.

"Allow me to introduce our guests," said McInerney. "First," consulting a card, "Miss Hazel Claflin, Development Director of Westside General Hospital." Hazel smiled, to no applause. "Next, the director of the hospital, Dr. T. Graydon Stokes." He nodded his patrician head, inspiring a hiss. When the pudgy Podesta was named and identified as professional fund-raising counsel, more hissers, emboldened, joined in. He blinked rapidly, flushed.

McInerney stated the ground rules. "We are extending the courtesy of giving each speaker an opportunity to *briefly* explain his—or her—position, after which the floor will be thrown open to questions. I call on Dr. Stokes to begin."

With the aplomb for which he was noted, and which usu-

49

ally made him an effective mediator, Stokes took McInerney's place at the mike while she retired to the chair set apart from the others. "Ladies and gentlemen, friends of Westside General, of the medical school and research center . . ." He paused. "For I believe everyone here *is* a good friend of this unique community resource, whatever our current differences may be . . . I am proud to explain and describe the program in which we all have a stake; and when you have heard me out I am sure that in your fairness and objectivity you will agree that the pluses far outweigh the few minuses"

He continued in this sweetly reasonable vein, eliciting coughs, foot shufflings and loud yawns from a body that plainly was not interested in being objective—and probably even less in being fair. I thought he made a good case for expansion . . . the pressure for more hospital beds in the age of AIDS, drugs and resurgent TB, the need for increased facilities to train tomorrow's doctors and the challenge posed by scientific progress to create additional space for research. But then, it was not my view of the Hudson or the midtown skyline that was about to be obliterated. And people had paid a lot for those views.

Stokes resumed his seat, in silence broken by a shouted challenge: "I have it on good authority that Krinsky is experimenting with leprosy bacteria! How do we know that all of us in this city are not at risk?"

I realized with a sinking feeling that this was a question I, if anybody, should answer; Krinsky was my special bailiwick and my job was to defend its fair name. Moreover, I was up on the leprosy project, having been briefed during my get-acquainted tour of the building. Fortunately, I was spared from having to take on the challenger—for the moment at least: McInerney, again at the mike, held up her hand. "Good question! But let's save it and others until all three have spoken. Now, Miss Claflin, please."

As Hazel stepped to the lectern her calm demeanor was not, I knew, an expression of how she felt. "I used to work on a newspaper," she said, "and I quickly learned to suspect all words spoken in public. But I also learned that there are occasions when people in positions of trust must tell the truth or good things cannot come to pass and bad ones will get worse." Drawing on her reporter's skills she illustrated Stokes's points in their human interest aspects—dramatizing the benefits of expansion in terms of individuals and families. In spite of themselves, her hearers paid attention. Even so, when she sat down, they still couldn't bring themselves to give her a polite hand.

Podesta was defeated before he started; the earlier hissing, and his blushing reaction to it, had weakened him. He made the further mistake of opening on a defensive note: "I wanted to show you some architects' drawings and some slides of present conditions that need correcting, but I wasn't permitted." Before he could go on, a lout jumped up to demand, "How much are you professional bloodsuckers creaming off the money that comes in?" And as Podesta turned to Madam Chairperson, expecting her to call the heckler to order, the next jab landed: "You're sure not in this for your health!"

"Or ours!" chimed in a woman from across the floor.

"Let him speak!" cried a man but he was booed down. Another man stood up, a six-footer, strong featured, fifty-five or so, and issued a one-word command: "*Quiet!*" His powerful presence and voice restored calm.

"Who's that?" I asked a fellow standee.

"Warrenton," he said. "Wallace Warrenton. Dynamo, that guy. He and Stokes used to be friends."

Podesta began again, this time trying to answer the question about fund raisers' take. The question showed a lack of knowledge, he said. Ethical professionals do not get a percentage of what comes in, they provide their service for a fee set according to the guidelines of the American Association of Fundraising Counsel. Thus whatever is contributed by the public goes straight into the campaign fund.

"That's just semantics!" objected a shrill woman in the front row. Podesta ignored her and plowed on, citing examples of large subscriptions to the present campaign that indicated substantial popular support. Next he played what obviously was meant to be his trump card: "The first hospital in this country was the Pennsylvania Hospital—and that got built *because Benjamin Franklin went around soliciting subscriptions from public-spirited fellow citizens like yourselves!*"

It fell on deaf ears. No one was listening—conversations

51

had broken out all around, and McInerney unceremoniously took over the mike and opened the question period.

The guy with the thing about leprosy was back. To show off his savvy he initiated the new attack by first referring to the disorder as "Hansen's disease, commonly known as leprosy." Then: "Can someone give me one good reason why this condition, rare in our society and extremely contagious, should be deliberately introduced into our midst? As we know in spite of all the official assurances we've had about nuclear safety, the ozone layer etcetera etcetera, no one tells the truth if they have an ax to grind. So let's think for ourselves! Let's recognize that there's no completely foolproof way of confining a disease to a laboratory or a hospital bed. The possible spread of leprosy is enough to make any sane person say no to giving the Krinsky Research Center more space and more power than it already has!"

The members of our beleaguered trio on the platform looked at one another. How to answer such a farrago of garble, error and fuzzy thinking? I moved away from the wall into center aisle and spoke up.

"I'd like to reply to the gentleman. My name is Bert Swain, I'm with Krinsky—my job is to explain to the public what we do there and why. First of all, Hansen's disease [I used the less familiar term as being less threatening] is *not* extremely contagious. It's transmitted only by prolonged, intimate contact. Immigrants from the third world are bringing it into this country, so by treating and studying some of the carriers Krinsky is doing what it can to contain Hansen's—not spread it! Furthermore, Hansen's is closely related to TB, which we know is on the rise. The way the host defends itself in both diseases is similar, many of the cells that kill the bacteria are the same. Anything we learn about fighting Hansen's should help us fight tuberculosis. Therefore, contrary to what we've just heard, Krinsky deserves all the support it can get!"

My heart was racing, my throat had gone dry. I'd made what was probably too much of a speech but I thought it was convincing. I looked to the stage and got a flicker of a smile from Hazel. Stokes, too, appeared approving. But I might as well not have spoken. Ignoring the points I'd made, a sharp-faced woman got up to continue the attack on Krinsky:

"Don't think we've forgotten the executive at Krinsky who got fired for stealing! That would have been just the tip of the iceberg! And now with all the building-fund money to steal from—"

Another woman rose from her seat. "I take exception to that!" she said in a don't-mess-with-me tone. Her voice was of considerable size for someone of small stature. "I'm the new comptroller at Krinsky—the one who discovered the padded purchase orders and fired the guilty party. He's now serving time. And I can assure you that in my part of the medical center every penny we take in or pay out is accounted for!"

On the stage Dr. Stokes got to his feet. "Thank you, Mrs. Silversmith. Let me add that if anyone has any evidence of fiscal abuse in any part of Westside Medical Center I want to hear about it. But unsubstantiated charges . . . innuendoes . . . have no place in this discussion!"

"I'm a working mother," announced a fortyish female, "and I keep getting billed by the hospital for something I already paid!" She began a recital, chapter and verse, of failed attempts to set the record straight. Several other people with grievances started competing to be heard. Rebellion was simmering in the ranks. Soon there were angry words about picketing Westside, blocking delivery of supplies, filing suit for violations of city ordinances, not letting 'them' get away with it! An ominous hum emerged from many throats . . . the sound of a crowd potentially out of control.

I signaled to Hazel and pantomimed getting the hell out. She stood, moved to Stokes's side and whispered something. They left the platform via the backstage route, Podesta trailing.

I slipped through the rear doors, fearful that the crowd might try to detain my party, determined to reach them first and help them escape. But as I was hurrying along the corridor someone suddenly shoved me from behind. Catching myself, I swung around. Before I saw my assailant, I got a whiff of his hundred-proof breath. "Where ya think yer goin', motherfucker? We still got questions!" His sneer took up most of his ugly face.

"Keep your hands to yourself!"

"Who's gonna make me?"

I tried to remember the little I'd learned at Midtown Boxing. Actually, I wasn't taught anything about dealing with drunks. I was on my own. Whereas before instruction I probably would have delivered a half-hearted swipe, I let the bastard have it with my balled fist to the midriff—full force. He fell back with a surprised "Aaghh!" Would he now lunge at me like a wounded tiger, and if so how would I deal with it? If he was any good, I couldn't see myself winning.

He didn't lunge, however. With a baleful look he pulled himself together. "Don't think yer gonna get away with this, shit head!" Then, to my vast relief, he turned and stumbled back in the direction he'd come from. I felt good and would have felt elated, except that he was so sodden I was pretty sure that was the only reason I'd prevailed.

Hazel and Dr. Stokes, however, had just been emerging from backstage when this little drama took place. They saw me hit the guy and saw him retreat. How could they help being impressed? When Hazel introduced me to her boss, he took my hand and said, "You were splendid—out here and in there. Simply splendid."

Podesta, just catching up with the others, looked nonplussed, but no one was paying attention to him.

"Now that you're in safe hands," Stokes told Hazel, "I must be getting home."

"Certainly. Take care."

"You were good too."

"Thank you."

I wanted to go some place with Hazel where we could hash over what had just happened at the meeting. I knew she had the same idea. Podesta, sensing what we had in mind and hoping to be in on it, lingered after Stokes's departure.

"Be talking to you, Ben," said Hazel. "Tomorrow."

He took the hint. "Sure. Good night."

We goodnighted him out.

"Where to?" Hazel asked.

"Not around here—wouldn't want to run into any of these yahoos."

"There's a coffee shop near my place. You can get a drink."

Flushed by my success at the manly art, I said, "My trainer told me to lay off the hard stuff. Coffee'll be fine."

"Your trainer!"

"Well, instructor. I *am* taking boxing lessons."

"Now I've heard everything."

We started down the hall toward the building entrance, hoping we wouldn't get waylaid as we left. There was hubbub from the auditorium—apparently COMCE had enough going on to keep the mob happily occupied without us. As we were passing the auditorium doors, Silversmith, the comptroller, popped out.

"Oh, good! I was just coming to look for you—I was afraid there'd be trouble."

"There almost was," said Hazel, "but Bert took care of it— with his fists."

Silversmith regarded me with, I thought, a certain respect. "Hi, Bert. I'm Eve." I took the hand she extended. She was compactly put together—not skinny but firm. Her brown hair was piled in a coil, probably to add height. Her eyes, too, were brown, and sparkling. She was wearing a sweater and a short skirt—okay even for a woman who looked to be about my age, because she had a girl's legs. "Fists *and* words. You gave that character whatfor about the leprosy."

"You weren't so bad yourself.

"So many yahoos in one place—scary!" said Eve. Yahoos again; I had no monopoly on the word. Hazel and I exchanged glances. I could see her wheels turning; Eve and I were on the same beam, she was thinking. So I wasn't totally unprepared when *my* friend invited *her* friend to come along to the coffee shop. She'd been dying to fix me up with somebody, and here was her chance.

After we'd discussed what had gone on at the school, Eve remarked, "I'd expected the opposition would be strong, but not that it'd be so . . . so full of hate."

That struck a chord with me. "You probably know that one of our lab scientists is missing."

"Yes, Faith Frawley."

"Well, tonight I saw something: the capacity for potential violence in people who probably live peaceable lives day by day. It made me understand—really understand at a gut level—how Faith might have been done in by someone she knew . . . or thought she did. Someone who'd never indicated a bent for murder."

A silence followed this. Then Eve asked, "Do you have any idea who such a person might be? I'm not asking for a name," she added quickly.

"No. But it gives me something to think about."

"I heard you're working on the case. I pick up a lot about what goes on at Krinsky . . . being in the money department puts you at the nerve center. If you need information and I have it and am at liberty to talk, maybe I can help."

"Thank you. I might take you up on it."

"Now I've got to go." She picked up her purse from the seat.

"Eve lives on the East Side near where you are," said Hazel. "You could share a taxi."

Eve spoke before I could. "That would be lovely, but I'm afraid not. I've promised to drop in on a friend on West Eighty-fifth."

Since we refused to accept her money for a vodka on the rocks, Eve left a tip for the three of us.

"Quite a lady," said Hazel. "What do you think?"

"I agree. Terrific. But she's not my type."

"I know your types. A string of doozies."

"But thanks for trying," I said. I sipped what was left of my cooled-off, unappetizing coffee.

My idea of what constituted my type was shortly to undergo revision.

SIX

Phones used to ring, now they burble. If I'm going to be roused from sleep at five forty-five a.m., I'd rather it were by the old startling *br-r-r-ing* than this insidious liquidy sound that slithers into your sleep and gradually irritates you awake.

On this particular morning when I picked up the phone by the bed, it was Darryl Cromart on the line—though it took me a minute to recognize him. He was in a state.

"Get over to Krinsky right away!" Then something about "body." I'd missed the first couple of sentences.

"What about a body?" I was sitting up straight, straining to hear.

"Security—they just called. A body in the delivery area."

"Whose?"

"I don't know. Can't touch anything till the police arrive."

"Have they been called?"

"Yes—on the way."

"I'll be right over!"

Fifteen minutes later I jumped out of a cab. The delivery area was what my office overlooked. One half of the iron gate to the street stood open. A uniformed cop barred my way until I showed him my Westside Medical Center I.D.

Cromart had beat me by a couple of minutes. This morning he had paid no attention to his appearance. His usually sleek silver hair was disorderly, his slacks and jacket didn't go together and he needed a shave, as did I. Another policeman in uniform stood guard near by. The body, a little beyond Cromart, was face down, left arm bent under it, the right out at an angle, palm up. It was clothed in expensive-looking glen plaid.

"It's Morgan Dixon," Cromart greeted me, in a horrified

whisper. "He"—indicating the cop—"took the wallet out of his back pocket. There was I.D."

Dr. Dixon had presided over a laboratory one floor up from mine across the court. His private office enjoyed the luxury of a small terrace decked out with white plastic table and chairs. During these summer days members of his staff lolled outside where sunshine and furtive breezes occasionally crept in through gaps in the concrete. The lollers had my envy.

I glanced up now at the terrace. "How—" I started to ask.

"There're two detectives up there looking around," said Cromart.

In addition to the terrace there were four windows that seemed to belong to the lab. At the moment all were closed.

"Any idea whether he jumped—or . . . ?" As I asked, it occurred to me that he might have died somewhere else and been dumped here. Obviously Cromart, shaking his head, knew no more than I did.

Emergency vehicles, like telephones, make a different noise these days. Sirens once wailed. Now they whoop and cackle. Something laughing maniacally could be heard speeding through the streets toward us. Soon a van drew into the yard and three men got out: one, sharp-faced, forty or so, in a business suit, the others white-coated, unloading a stretcher. Immediately after them came a step van containing a police mobile crime laboratory and crew, they being followed by a reporter and a photographer.

Once pictures were taken of the body, the sharp-featured man moved forward and rolled it over. Cromart and I now knew for sure we were looking at the face of Morgan Dixon, sickeningly smashed.

My morning's work had begun.

It was to go on at a hectic pace for the next few hours. This was one story I had no hope of sweeping under the rug. It was also one I had no way to soft-pedal, nor could I prevent speculation about a possible murder since no suicide note had been found. Among the media types on the scene only one, from ABC Television news, was someone I knew, and he was in no position to do me or the center any favors.

A meeting of Westside brass from all divisions—hospital,

medical school and center—was called for ten-thirty. It was held in a large conference room on Cromart's designer floor. I was in and out of it, having to leave several times when Altagracia came to fetch me. News organizations I'd never heard of had got wind of what had happened and had to be dealt with.

Needing to know what went on when I wasn't at the meeting, I arranged to have lunch with Hazel in the hospital cafeteria. She'd been present throughout.

We unloaded our trays and sat down, both of us weary. I knew Hazel had been hard hit: Dixon had been chairman of the campaign committee that solicited contributions from Krinsky's top echelon of scientists. His death left a big hole.

"You missed one interesting thing," said Hazel. "Stokes brought it up." Westside General's director had raised the question of whether Dixon might have met his fate at the hands of a person or persons opposed to the expansion program.

"That's crossed my mind," I said.

"Mine too."

"And what was the reaction?"

"A little hard to read. I sensed a reluctance to think in those terms. These people don't like the idea that community hostility could go that far."

"They should have been at the school the other night!"

"They'd much rather, if it was murder, that it was some personal score being settled. Then everybody active in the campaign wouldn't feel threatened."

"If they do believe Dixon was killed for being committee chairman," I said, "it might be hard to find someone willing to replace him."

"Actually," Hazel said, "it would be stupid of the killer to pull the same stunt again. That would make it easier to catch him. So a replacement shouldn't be running any special risk."

"Logical, but try telling that to your candidate. He or she may not be convinced."

"She," echoed Hazel. "Thanks for that."

"For what?"

"I'd forgotten. Emily Norton. She was our first choice before we asked Dixon."

"She turned it down?"

"Her husband was sick and it looked like a long recovery. But I hear he's better now. I think maybe she could be persuaded."

I was aware of Dr. Norton's reputation in AIDS research, also of her ability to attract money for that from highly placed friends. "Could it be that she'd rather just raise money for AIDS?"

"Her husband was really sick. I think she was telling the truth when she didn't take the job. We can try her again."

I now brought up something that was nagging at me and refused to go away, even though I had nothing to support it. "Would you think I was being weird if I said I have a feeling that Faith and Dixon—what's happened to them—is connected?"

"Connected, how?"

"I can't say. It's just a feeling."

Hazel ran it over in her mind. Then: "No. Not weird. Not at all. What are you planning to do about it?"

"What *can* I do about it? I don't seem to have got anywhere with Faith, and the police are probably doing whatever needs to be done about Dixon."

"Maybe, maybe not."

I suddenly remembered the strong-voiced man at the protest rally commanding "Quiet!" I'd been told his name was Wallace Warrenton and that he and Stokes "used to be friends." Presumably the building campaign had come between them. If I wanted to get a line on who might have eliminated one of the biggest fund raisers, I ought to talk to Warrenton.

"I do plan to do something about it," I said. "Thanks for the push." We were finished with our sandwiches; I was eager to be off and running. I stood. "I'll tell you about it later."

"Up and at 'em, kid."

In the hall outside my office I ran into one of the detectives who'd been on the case this morning. He introduced himself as Jerry Joyce. "You're Mr. Swain? Got a couple of minutes?"

I invited him in. He was about my age, of medium height, stocky, with wavy reddish-brown hair. He wore a gold wedding band and a bold necktie I pictured a fond wife picking out for him. When we were seated facing across my desk he said, "We're interviewing everybody who works in the center. Purely routine. I hope you don't mind answering a few questions." He took a pad out of his pocket to make notes.

So here I was, answering, not asking, for a change. "Anything you want."

"How well did you know Dr. Dixon?"

"Not very. I've only been here since the end of May."

"Would you say he was popular?"

"Respected, from what I've heard. I've met people on his staff but I don't know them well either, so I can't tell how they feel about him. Other scientists seem to think he does—did—good work."

"Would you know of any enemies?"

"Not specifically—but he was the head of an important committee raising funds for our expansion program and a lot of the neighbors are against it."

"Yes, I've heard. But the fact that he's gone won't stop the program, will it?"

"I shouldn't think so. There are other people on the committee and there'll probably be a new chairman."

"Have you ever been in his lab?"

"Once when I first came. I made a point of calling on all the lab chiefs . . . asking what they were doing . . . letting them know I was here to help."

"Help with what?"

"Well, as Director of Media Relations I interpret what goes on in the center to the public. My job is to keep the press and TV and radio informed and the scientists happy."

He nodded. "I saw you talking to the reporters. This kind of story can't make anybody happy around here."

I took the initiative. "You were up in Dixon's lab. Did you come across anything significant?"

He shrugged. "If we did, we don't know yet. Dusted for prints . . . checked with the staff if anything was missing. No signs of violence."

"Any theory whether suicide or murder?"

"Medical examiner may have something to say."

I felt he preferred to keep the questioning in his corner,

but I had one more thing to ask: "Did anyone happen to mention that one of the scientists in another lab here disappeared a few weeks ago?"

"Dr. Frawley—that her name?"

"Right."

"She's another precinct."

"Do you think there might be some connection between Frawley and what happened to Dixon?"

"Connection? Do you know something that links them?"

"No. It just seemed . . ."

I could see that my attempt to turn the Dixon case into something bigger wasn't getting very far. From a practical angle, it doubtless made sense for the police to keep their eyes on the immediate problem and avoid getting led into byways that, more likely than not, were dead ends.

As for dead ends, Sgt. Joyce evidently concluded that he and I had reached one. He got up, thanked me for my time, said he might be calling on me again, and left.

I followed him as far as the anteroom where Altagracia, on the phone, was assuring someone that no, there were no further developments. When she rang off, I asked her to see if she could find Wallace Warrenton in the phone book. I wanted to talk to him.

He was not an easy man to get an appointment with, but when his secretary relayed the information that I was Director of Media Relations at Krinsky his curiosity must have been aroused. Could I be an emissary seeking to calm troubled waters . . . perhaps bearing some kind of compromise proposal regarding the expansion program? That's how I imagined the mental process that led him to pick up the phone himself and make a date for three tomorrow afternoon.

After I'd gone this far I had a couple of second thoughts. One: I might be doing just the opposite of calming the waters if I voiced the suspicion that someone in Warrenton's camp had committed murder. Two: Shouldn't I clear this interview with Dr. Stokes, who might object to it? And if he didn't object, wouldn't it be a good idea for him to brief me about his former friend before I met him?

Stokes listened attentively as I explained my plan. I didn't tell him what I'd heard about the friendship gone sour; he brought it up himself: "Wally and I used to be friends, you know. At one time he was on the hospital board, but a few years ago when we started talking about expansion, he came down hard against it. He has a magnificent river view now, and he'd lose a piece. That would still leave him with an unobstructed vista all the way down to the Battery, but that's not enough. When he saw the votes were against him, he resigned and headed up the opposition. I was sorry; I liked the man. Still do. I can assure you anything like murder over something like this would be beyond him."

"But can we be sure about the others who are opposed?"

"I'm afraid not. We don't even know who they all are."

"So if I talk to Warrenton I might get a lead . . . the name of someone capable of . . ."

"Perhaps."

He wasn't raising the objection I'd feared, about my stepping out of line, stirring up more trouble. I asked what business Warrenton was in. Economic analysis and research—his own company. Consultant to major corporations. Self-made man, just missed being on the Olympic swimming team.

Taking my leave, I walked down the hall, one of Stokes's statements echoing in my brain. It struck me as odd: ". . . anything like murder over something like this would be beyond him."

Did that imply that in a situation involving something *un*-like this Warrenton might be a potential murderer?

SEVEN

The address was Wall Street—a high floor with the Statue of Liberty out the window. Warrenton did go for views. Darryl Cromart's corner office had been paneled in walnut; this one was in more stylish ash. Instead of sinking into deep-piled broadloom you walked gingerly on a patterned, multihued carpet that looked to be Turkish, worn thin by the footsteps of hundreds of years. I could see servitors bearing trays of jewels across the precious rug to the massive, carved desk yards away, for the master's approval.

Actually, as he rose to receive me, Warrenton didn't seem especially intimidating. If anything, he tended to be diminished in scale by the outsize proportions of the room. Since the desk was too wide to reach across and he didn't come around it, a handshake was dispensed with. He nodded me to the nearest leather chair. Retrieving a half-smoked cigar from a heavy crystal ashtray, he brought his hand to rest on a humidor and asked if I'd care to join him.

"Sorry, I gave them up." I *was* sorry. If it hadn't been for trying to meet my guru Michael's standards for boxers, I might have broken down and indulged in a smoke the way I sometimes sneaked a drink. But today was one of the days Michael was on deck as my superego. I could tell by the aroma when Warrenton puffed that this would have been a cigar the likes of which had not been available to the likes of me since Castro came to power.

Seated once more, Warrenton asked, "You've been sent by . . . whom?"

"It's not quite that way. I'm here on my own, about Dr. Dixon."

"Shocking, what happened." A pause while he looked me

64

over. "May I ask what your connection is . . . and what it's got to do with me?"

"I'm hoping you may be able to help clear up the mystery."

"Whether he jumped, fell or was pushed? Is that it?"

"Yes. And why."

"I certainly don't know. And I still don't understand your role. Are you licensed as a detective?"

"I handle the center's public relations. Until we can tell the world the truth about Dr. Dixon's death, Krinsky will be under a cloud. Did one of his colleagues or lab workers do him in? Could it have been somebody who wanted to derail the building program? He was one of its biggest fund raisers and as we both know there's a lot of opposition."

Warrenton's face suddenly purpled. "Are you suggesting that—"

"I'm not suggesting anything or anybody," I said hastily. God knows I hadn't meant to give the impression *he* was under suspicion. I tried to recover. "People are entitled to their opinion, but any group can have its fanatics. If there's someone so hellbent on blocking the program that he'd kill, we've got to find out who it is!"

"And I might be in a position to identify him, right?" This was said with such vehemence that I knew we were heading for a blowup—and no turning back.

"Please don't think—" I began. "The idea that you yourself—The last thing Dr. Stokes said to me was that it was inconceivable that you personally—" Saying all the wrong things.

Warrenton was on his feet. "So Stokes is behind this!"

"No! I simply let him know I was coming here!"

"I've heard enough! Get the hell out of my office!"

He bore down on me and, against all common sense, I held my ground.

"I'll leave," I said. "But if you touch me, I'll sue!"

That stopped him. If my threat was a bluff, he didn't dare call it. The possibility of his name being splashed all over the media—and it would be—evidently didn't appeal to him.

Going down in the elevator I realized the publicity would probably be even worse for me. My employers would take a very dim view of it. I was getting off lucky.

65

Meanwhile, Randi. Sharkey's, where we'd picked each other up, was out as a rendezvous; Clyde might still be after us—he'd phoned a couple of times, she reported, and she'd hung up on him. So we met at other places and afterward went to my apartment instead of hers.

The sex was still good . . . better than good, but it turned out to carry a price tag. When I called Randi to set up our second get-together, she said, "I want to have dinner at that restaurant you were planning to take that girl to."

"Why there?"

"Why? You were gonna try to get into her pants so it must have been expensive."

"If you want, sure."

We went. It *was* expensive.

She also wanted to see the latest Broadway musical smash (sixty-five smackeroos per ticket plus broker's fees) and to go dinner-dancing at the Rainbow Room. I weaseled out of the latter; a trial sashay in my apartment, where I made myself trip over my feet and hers, convinced her I was no dancer. She was given to stopping in front of jewelers' windows, her arm linked in mine, and pointing out what she liked. She had a birthday coming up.

Something told me our affair had a fairly short life expectancy—about as short as my bank balance after paying bills, rent and child support.

The night of my encounter with Warrenton I woke up, Randi in bed beside me, to find that I was host to an idea. Apparently it had crept into my head while I was asleep. What did I know about Faith and Gordon's research? I'd been told something when I first arrived and made the rounds; now, trying to remember what it was, I drew a blank. The same for what Dixon had been doing or supervising. Well, if there was, as I'd theorized, a link between the twin mysteries of Faith and Dixon, might it relate to what they'd been working on? I resolved to look into it tomorrow—or, rather, today—and settled down to go back to sleep.

I was too keyed up by my idea's potential, however, and it wasn't until around seven o'clock that I fell into a doze. Randi poked me awake just before eight. We dressed and downed coffee in a rush. No gym for me this morning.

Dragging groggily into my office, past ever-fresh Altagracia, I crossed to the window and looked down to see if there were any new bodies. Not a one.

The Dixon laboratory suite had the air of a funeral parlor when I walked in a little later. In the big room off to the side white-coated workers were going about their business with sagging shoulders and unsmiling faces. Also depressed-looking was Dixon's secretary, at her desk in the reception area. I remembered her from my first visit, a handsome young black woman, but not her name. It was spelled out on a clear plastic strip facing me: Deborah Jaynes. Jaynes's mental files were better organized than Swain's; she knew *my* name and my position on the Krinsky organization chart.

I accepted her invitation to have a seat. "How are you people getting along?"

"We're still in a state of shock."

"Is somebody taking charge?"

She shook her head. "Not yet. Everybody's going on doing what they were when Dr. Dixon . . . I'm still getting out letters he dictated. I've canceled two conferences he was planning to attend. One of them he was going to chair."

"I don't want to add to your load," I said, "but do you have some kind of list of research projects in this lab? I may have to answer questions about what goes on here and how it'll be affected by what's happened."

"Well, we did get something together a few weeks ago. Projects and protocols. I can give you a copy—nothing basic has changed."

"I'd appreciate it."

Back in my office, I opened the folder I'd been handed and scanned the page listing the titles of studies under way: "A New Transporter of Anti-cancer Drugs in Cancer Cell Membranes," "Recombinant Expression of a Novel Isoform of P Glycoprotein," "Deletion of the Gene for a Novel Anti-cancer Drug Transporter by Homologous Recombination" and several other grabbers. I might as well come clean and admit that the following dozen or so pages with the protocols describing the researchers' strategies were not immediately intelligible to me. In order to tell anyone what they were about I would have to go to the investigators themselves and have them explain things in simpler terms. That was how I had operated as a reporter on the science beat, and I'd managed to get by.

Now, however, in order to understand as much as I could before bothering the workers, I took the folder into the science library, located in the main hospital building. There I read the entire report carefully with the aid of dictionaries, encyclopedias, textbooks and copies of *Science, Nature, The Journal of Experimental Medicine, Scientific American* and whatever else the librarian could recommend. I spent the rest of the day that way, ending up with some glimmer of what each group in Dixon's lab was trying to achieve.

Tomorrow I would go through a similar routine involving Wells's lab, concentrating particularly on what Faith and Gordon had been exploring. If I could detect any relationship between what any of the Wells and Dixon teams were working on, I'd turn to them for clarification. It might be there was a rivalry between labs, a race to get a certain answer first. It was hard to believe that such a race could lead to murder; but when you thought about it, the reasons people killed other people often seemed insufficient—even trifling—to the bystander.

My brain hadn't had so much exercise in a long time, and I started the next day punchy. When I explained my plan to Dr. Wells, he gave me what I thought was a skeptical look over his half-mast specs. But he said, "Why not?" His secretary got up a kit of stuff from his lab, including a few published papers, some progress reports and several grant applications that had led to funding.

Back to the library where I passed the better part of another day.

I started with Faith and Gordon. Their experiments were concerned with oncogenes, which I figured out are substances that transform healthy cells into cancerous cells. After skimming the explanation of what they were trying to accomplish, I took a second look at the descriptions of the various cancer-related studies under way in Dixon's lab. No real connection or overlap that I could see between them and what Faith and Gordon were doing; nor were other projects going forward under Wells's supervision any closer in content to the Dixon projects.

I pushed everything I'd been studying to the far edge of the table and leaned back in my chair, unwinding from being hunched over so long. I'd established one thing to my satisfaction: the Wells and Dixon contingents appeared to be neither cooperating nor competing in their research.

But might they, I wondered, be competing in some other area? For space or equipment in the new quarters now on the drawing board? Or for funding? Despite modest increases in the budget of the National Institutes of Health, money from that source for basic research seemed to have slowed to a trickle. Foundations that supported science, and even pharmaceutical companies, were keeping a tighter grip on their pursestrings. Scientists who felt—or thought they felt—the ground giving way under their feet might be driven to desperate measures to save their laboratories and themselves.

The person who would know the financial status of the various Krinsky labs—where their dollars came from, and who had applied for what grants—would be Eve Silversmith. Her office—"the money department"—was, as she'd said, the nerve center; an institution like Krinsky always took a hefty percentage of everything that came in for overhead, and she was the one keeping track. So she was bound to have a good idea of which researchers were in trouble.

I was glad I'd met Eve the night of the protest meeting. Her offer to help had been genuine.

If nothing prevented it, like another death or disappearance, I'd call on her tomorrow.

EIGHT

Eve was bustling about in a dark-gray pantsuit, a colorful paisley at her throat, long earrings swinging dramatically, when I arrived in her office to keep my appointment. Directing the work of a couple of assistants, she was completely in charge.

We withdrew into her private office where I explained what I wanted to find out. She told me that teams in both labs—Dixon's and Wells's—had applied to the same source, the Staley Foundation, for renewal of existing grants; and without referring to the files she was able to cite the different dates for the periods to be covered and the amounts requested. Further, she volunteered the information that Staley was planning to cut back on its largesse and her contact there had advised her they were going to have to eliminate funding for one or the other of the two studies.

I asked, "Can you tell me who's on the Wells team?"

"Faith Frawley—if she turns up again—and Gordon Barnard."

Maybe I *was* on the track of something. "And who's on the Dixon team?"

She mentioned three names, then added, "Dr. Dixon was listed too."

I recalled the Dixon project as the one about deletion of a gene for a novel anti-cancer drug transporter by homologous recombination.

"Could you say which grant stood a better chance of being continued?"

"Not really."

"But after Frawley disappeared . . . do you think maybe Dixon gained the advantage?"

She considered this. "I don't know. Certainly his team should have been in a stronger position than before."

"Then later, with Dixon dead, the balance might have shifted back again?"

She gave me a searching look. "Are you saying that what happened to Frawley and Dixon . . . ?"

I had quickly decided that with this smart lady there was no point in playing games.

"There's a lot at stake in these two laboratories," I said. "I have no idea whether Faith Frawley is still alive. I'm afraid maybe not. There's a strong possibility Dr. Dixon was murdered, and if so my hunch is it might have been over those grants."

"And Faith might have been murdered first?"

"I realize it's hard to conceive that people connected with this center could be so inhuman."

Was I being inexcusably rash, confiding such suspicions to someone I barely knew? What if she started blabbing and word got back to the two labs? A case could easily be made that I was poisoning the atmosphere at the center. Yet I felt in my bones I could trust her.

"All too human," she said in response to my statement, then went on: "It may interest you to know that three labs are doing their damnedest to get the same space in the new construction. It's bigger than what any of them has now."

"I suppose two of the labs are Dixon and Wells."

She nodded. "The third's Dr. Latner."

I'd met Philip Latner on my early rounds and had seen him at the meeting called after Dixon's death, where he sat mostly silent. One of the projects in his lab was to develop an improved treatment for leprosy. It was he who had brought me up to date on the disease's growing incidence in the U.S.

Now that I'd decided Eve could be trusted, I felt free to ask my next question: "Is it possible that Latner might kill for the best lab on the block?"

She looked at me deadpan for a minute, then glanced at the watch on her wrist. "We seem to have established in six and a half minutes that practically anyone around here is capable of practically anything."

I set up an appointment to see Latner that afternoon. I promised his secretary to keep it short.

For a man probably not out of his forties he had a patriarchal air: serious dark beard threaded with gray, gold-rimmed glasses through which wisdom (or an approximation thereof) gazed speculatively, hands that seemed to shape each deliberate word on the desk before him as he spoke it. Family photographs surrounded him with what looked like scads of children, though they were probably just the same three or four at different stages.

I couldn't think of any decent way to put the question uppermost in my mind—the one I had asked Eve. The most I could do was try to lead him into saying something that might betray a potential killer.

He was waiting for me to justify my presence.

"I thought it was time to touch base with you again," I said. "Maybe you've got something going that's reached the point where we should let the public in on it?"

"Mm. Let me think." He swiveled to look out the window. After a moment he said, "I've got two people working on a study of Hansen's disease and leishmaniasis. They've come up with some interesting observations, but it's all still pretty preliminary."

"Leishmaniasis . . ." I tried to recall what I knew about it. "That has some symptoms like Hansen's, doesn't it?"

He nodded. "It's a parasitical infection transmitted by sand flies. We're especially concerned with the American variety."

"I talked to someone about it when I was just starting here."

"Well, we're not ready to announce anything just yet."

"Can't be hurried of course."

"We *are* on the threshold of a couple of other things. I think it's going to be a good year for our group."

"But nothing, at this point, to tell the world about."

"Right. I'm glad to know you're keeping tabs—I'll certainly let you know when we're far enough along . . ."

I sailed, I thought, smoothly on. "Are you going to be moving into the new construction? Better space?"

His face darkened. "Are we sure there's going to *be* new construction?"

"The plans are firm, money's coming in."

"It has been. Only, the community's throwing up road-blocks. And now we've lost the chairman of one of our key committees."

"Tragic," I acknowledged, "but don't you think everyone's going to work that much harder?" I tried to look reflective. "In a worst-case scenario, if we had to drop the expansion program, I suppose you'd still be happy with what you've got here. You seem to be getting results . . . important results."

"Happy!" The sage-like calm of couple of minutes ago had totally vanished. "How can a person be happy with all the intrigue that's going on?"

"Intrigue?"

"People trying to undercut you—take away what's yours—"

"I had no idea. . . ."

"Don't misunderstand. Dixon's death was deplorable. But some of the tricks he was pulling . . . I've been complaining about the inadequacies of this laboratory for years, and finally the building committee promised me what I needed in the new construction. But the latest word . . . Dixon was in line to get it!"

"Why?"

"Why? It was obvious—a payoff for the campaign pledges he was screwing out of the rest of us! I'm practically buying that laboratory! And now that he's dead they'll probably name it after him and give it to whoever they appoint to succeed him!"

I thought *You didn't think about that when you were getting rid of him, did you?* Then I had to admit I had nothing to back up such an accusation. If Latner really had killed, wouldn't he have kept his bitterness hidden?

Who could tell? Sometimes criminals want to give them-selves away—or at least tempt fate, sending messages that could betray their guilt but counting on people being too blind to decode them.

After leaving Latner it occurred to me that it would make sense to check whether he or Wells, or someone from one of their labs, had been in the center after regular hours on the night Dixon took the plunge. There was always a security guard on duty and after seven p.m. everyone using the main entrance had to sign in or out. The trouble was that the center could also be entered or left via the passage connecting with the hospital, a route that was not monitored. So even if the log book didn't carry a name from one of the two labs, it wouldn't mean that someone associated with them hadn't been in the building.

For whatever it might be worth, I went downstairs to talk to the guard. He informed me that the police had already checked the record of comings and goings. If they'd discovered anything interesting, they'd kept it to themselves.

Was there something wrong with my detective work? I was finding things to be suspicious about but didn't seem to know how to extract evidence from them.

I soon had more to puzzle over. Faith's father phoned. His voice was so low that at first I couldn't tell who it was. When I finally caught on, I realized he was deeply despondent.

"I don't suppose you've heard anything since last time," he said. (I'd called the Frawleys about ten days ago to report no news.)

"I'm afraid not."

"Neither have the police."

He would be coming east next Tuesday to clear out Faith's apartment. Could I hire a moving company to pack her things while he supervised, and arrange for their shipment home? I promised to set it up. I asked how he and Mrs. Frawley were. He said tonelessly, "We're living day to day," and added, "I'll be coming alone this time."

In a way it seemed as though more than a month had passed since I'd first met them and, hoping against hope, he'd written a check for the July rent. At the same time it felt like last week . . . maybe because there'd been no progress and I wanted to believe that in almost a month we'd surely have learned something.

The day he was planning to arrive would be July twenty-ninth; the apartment would be ready for a new tenant August first.

I asked Altagracia to engage the movers. When she said

she had a cousin in the business, I felt relieved; I was sure she'd get Frawley a fair deal.

I also asked Fumi and Gordon if they'd be willing to help Frawley with his desolate task. Both agreed to.

On the appointed morning I looked into their lab and was reassured to see no sign of either; they'd gone straight to Roosevelt Island. I decided that around noon I would join them.

The bed had just been knocked down and was being carried out by two muscular Latino youths when I reached the apartment door. Fumi was sitting on one of the deep window sills and Gordon, crosslegged, on the floor near by. He was smoking a cigarette, using a coffee container as an ashtray. There were eight or ten packing cases and a composition-board closet grouped toward the front of the room, ready for removal.

"We felt he wanted to be alone," said Fumi, sotto voce, inclining her head toward the bedroom.

"He's pretty broken up." Gordon, too, spoke softly.

I decided to wait for Frawley to emerge before letting him know I was here. The place looked emptier than I could have imagined, and sad. I leaned against the wall, noticing pale rectangles on the other walls where pictures had been taken down. Several minutes went by without our saying anything.

A low sound issued from the next room—like a cough, but choked.

After a while I went to the window and looked out. A high layer of cloud not dense enough to block the sun made for a glaring brightness. There was no river traffic at the moment. I reminded myself that the East River was not really a river; it was a channel—a tidal strait, as I'd read somewhere— connecting Upper New York Bay and Long Island Sound. Treacherous currents here and there; a famous one at Hell Gate, to the north where the East and Harlem Rivers joined. The view I had earlier thought attractive struck me as ominous, like an empty de Chirico street in which something seemed about to happen.

Frawley entered. He appeared even smaller now than when I had last seen him. I said hello, he thanked me for coming, I asked if there was anything I could do.

"I don't think—" he started to say, then thought of something: "If you'd turn in the keys for me after everything's out . . . That's something I'd just as soon . . ."

"Of course. Are you staying in town tonight? Maybe we could have dinner together."

"Thank you." He seemed pleased, as much as he could be under the circumstances, and for a minute I expected he was going to take me up on it. Then he shook his head. "I *was* going to fly back tomorrow, but with you handling the keys . . . If you could pay off the movers too . . . and bill me . . . I'll try to change my flight to this afternoon or tonight. I think Mother'd like to have me home."

"Certainly. Are you checked in at a hotel?"

"The Inter-Continental."

"Well, why don't you get back there now and make your new arrangements?"

"I think I'll do that."

No longer criticizing his daughter, just accepting the probability that he'd never see her again.

"I'll take care of everything."

"The young people have been of great help." He tried to smile at them.

"I'm afraid there wasn't very much . . ." Gordon demurred. He had got to his feet on Frawley's entrance, dousing the cigarette in the coffee container now in his hand. Fumi slipped from the windowsill to standing position.

Frawley addressed her: "Young lady, there's some of Faith's luggage in the bedroom. If you could use it . . ."

"I'll be glad to keep it for her."

As he was leaving, the movers came back. Fumi, Gordon and I trailed them into the bedroom where they hefted a chest of drawers. The luggage—two matching pieces, small, medium—stood in front of the bare, open closet. Fumi looked into the closet to make sure there was nothing left behind.

"It was a four-piece set," she said.

"I guess that's a hopeful sign, two missing," Gordon said. "Shows she packed."

"But those two were the big ones. And when I went through the clothes that are being shipped home I could swear she'd left almost everything behind. I knew what she owned. It was like she'd gone off with just what was on her back."

"You told me you and Faith weren't as close lately as you used to be," I reminded Fumi. "Couldn't she have bought new things you didn't know about?"

"Yes . . . I suppose so." But I didn't sense much conviction.

I had a call from Fumi that night. "I've been thinking," she began. "It isn't just those suitcases. . . ."

"No? What else?"

"Mr. Frawley wanted me to take whatever I wanted from the kitchen. I felt funny about it—I didn't want anything—but I went in and watched while they cleaned out the drawers and cupboards. And I noticed that there was only one casserole. It was part of a set—Creuset, you know those big orange-red ones—a set of three. The two biggest were gone. And it was the two biggest suitcases that were gone, too."

"Well, if she wasn't planning to come back—or at least not for a while—mightn't she have taken them?"

"The large sizes? Suitcases *and* casseroles? Unless she was planning to cook for a crowd of people, would it make sense to travel with pots that serve eight or ten? They're so heavy. Then, some new bath towels were gone. I'd been in Bloomie's with her the day she bought them on sale. It's all so strange."

"It does sound peculiar."

"Maybe I'm making too much out of it."

"You're a sharp observer. It works for you in the lab, I wouldn't discount it here." I remembered something. "That other time we went to Faith's apartment you noticed the frog bookends were missing."

"That's right. Maybe it all adds up."

There was a pause, then she said, "Faith is dead."

It took me a breath to reply, but I said, "I know."

NINE

Putting it into words, saying I knew Faith was dead, no longer taking it as just one possibility, had an effect on me. I felt something like sorrow, as though she'd been a friend—or at least an acquaintance,

I also felt a renewed urgency about learning who had killed her.

After my conversation with Fumi I spent a restless night (there'd been quite a few of those lately), and when I started working out at the gym next morning, Michael watched me for a while then motioned me over to a bench.

"The way you're holding your back," he said, in his Panamanian-flavored English. "You got any idea how tensed-up you are?"

I allowed as I did.

"What's bothering you, man?"

"A couple of murders."

He looked at me to judge if I was serious. He would have been perfectly willing to believe that I had killed two people and was having some kind of problem with it. I gathered Michael had seen a lot in his time.

"At least I think they're murders."

"Who got hit?"

"Man and a woman where I work. Woman's missing, man fell off a balcony—or was shoved."

"Maybe you better change jobs."

"My job now is to find out who did it."

"Isn't that one for the cops?"

"I'm trying to help them. They wish I'd get lost."

"So you're tied up in knots. My advice to you, amigo, is take a little time off—get away somewhere a few days, forget about it. You got a girlfriend?"

"Yeah, but if I take her with me it's going cost a bundle. Randi's got a black belt in shopping." Suddenly I thought of a place to go. A place I *should* go.

Deplaning at Pearson International late the next Saturday morning, I headed for a phone inside the terminal. At Doreen's hello I announced, "I made it." Doreen my former wife. We had arranged that if I arrived in Toronto on schedule I'd pick Paula up at her dancing class.

"How are you?" Doreen asked.

"Great." My voice a shade too bright. One went through these exchanges revealing as little as possible. "You okay?"

"Fine. What time do you think you'll drop her off later?"

"Well, if we do something after dinner . . ."

"Don't keep her out too late."

"How's Minnie?" Doreen's mother.

"She's wearing copper for her arthritis."

"Doesn't she know that's a superstition?"

"She read about it in *your* paper."

Touché. "My" paper was always *Inside Story,* never the more respectable *Record.* One of the reasons Doreen said she left me was that I didn't set high enough standards for myself. What really bugged her during those years of marriage was that I had started out with the idea of keeping my reporter's job only until I was a published novelist, after which, being a *successful* published novelist, I'd quit to write more books and we'd be up with the rich and famous. Only she didn't put it as crassly as that. Another reason she left me, and this was a real reason, was that she fell for another guy and thought he was going to divorce his wife and marry her. By the time it turned out he wasn't marrying her *she* had filed for divorce. At that point in her life Doreen had suffered three major disappointments: my lack of ambition (I never even finished one novel), abandonment by her lover and not making it professionally as a dancer. Having grown up in Toronto, and Minnie owning a house there, she had followed the path of least resistance and gone home to mother, taking Paula with her. All this before the *Record* folded. Now Doreen had a job with an insurance company.

"If I can come get Paula again in the morning," I said, "we could have breakfast at the hotel before I leave."

"That'll be up to her. And maybe after today you'll have had enough."

"Could be. Hello to Minnie."

I went to the car rental counter, was handed my keys. Minutes later, speeding along the straight flat highway, I was enjoying the weather—clearer and slightly cooler than what we'd been having down south. As I entered the city's outskirts I was reminded as always how civilizedly clean it was.

The dance studio was not far from where I was staying. I stopped at the hotel just long enough to check in, then headed for the old house off Yonge Street in which the class was held. Other parents in their cars were there ahead of me, mostly doubleparked; I joined their ranks. Soon girls, some younger, some older than Paula, began to emerge. Supple, fresh-faced, each carrying her little bag with leotard and slippers . . . I felt forbidden stirrings.

Paula was next to last. I would have liked it if she'd been out first, bursting with eagerness to see Daddy. As it was, she came forward onto the porch the opposite of eager. I got out of the car and hurried to meet her. I felt proud of how she looked: several inches taller than four—or was it five?—months ago when I'd last flown up, almost skinny, with pale hair frizzed in the current fashion. Her eyes, of unusual color, between amber and brown, were set off by pink-framed glasses. When she was a little older, her face more filled out, she would be beautiful. She was dressed in a tan poplin skirt and a blouse that almost matched her eyes.

"Hi, sweetheart." We met at the bottom step and she permitted a kiss to the forehead. "You look super." No comment. "Are you starving?"

"Mmm."

We started for the car. "Here, let me take your bag, I'll lock it in the trunk." I opened the door on her side, shut her in, went around to the rear and stowed the bag away. Even in the open air it seemed to give off a faint feminine fragrance.

Back behind the wheel, I asked, "Some place in particular for lunch? Down to Harborfront?"

She wrinkled her nose. "That's *boring*."

"Well, there's a nice restaurant in my hotel." I began to ease us out into traffic.

"Why don't we just have a cheeseburger or something?"
"Okay."
"We could get one at Eaton Center."
My antennae picked up the message. However attenuated our relationship had been on past visits, we had always somehow found our way to Eaton Center. Once there, Paula would shop. (Was she going to turn into a Randi?) To look at her, she never appeared to lack any essential, so perhaps the shopping was her way of making me pay—for more than mere merchandise.

Street parking was not to be had where we were going. I drove into a garage . . . up the ramp, around and around until we found a space at the top. Then down by elevator to the sidewalk, where I tried to float a conversation. How is school? . . . Do anything special over spring vacation? . . . Having a good time in dancing class? I was really concerned about the answer to this last, afraid Doreen might be trying to achieve dance stardom vicariously through Paula. I didn't want my daughter made victim of her mother's thwarted aspirations. But each of my questions drew the usual opaque answer.

When we entered the airy enclosed mall, Paula piloted me to the burger stand she had in mind. I could see that food was merely a preliminary to the real matter at hand.

"Is there something in one of the shops . . . ?"
This sparked her to life. "Rollerblades. All the kids have them."

What I'd seen of rollerblade skating made it look harder than the old-fashioned kind. And, for a dancer, dangerous?

"Have you been on rollerblades?"
"A friend of mine let me try hers. All I need is a little practice."

"But for a dancer . . . couldn't you get hurt?" As I asked I was thinking that if she wasn't worried about injury, then maybe that was a sign she could take her dancing or leave it.

"Oh, you wear knee guards and wrist guards and elbow pads and a helmet."

It began to sound pricey . . . but if this was the way to buy acceptance . . .

"Well, as soon as we finish lunch . . ."

Animated, she wolfed down the rest of her cheeseburger.

Even knowing I was about to be taken for more than I cared to spend, I welcomed her swing of mood. She was now almost friendly.

Rock assaulted our ears as we walked into the brightly lit shop. By the time we walked out again with a bag holding a couple of hundred bucks of gear, top of the line of course, I was telling myself that it was worth it to see those amber eyes alight. Furthermore . . . it was a bargain, really . . . Canadian dollars would be converted to American on my Amex bill.

Clutching her treasures, Paula planted a kissed on my cheek. My resentment at being suckered vanished. Okay, I was a sucker, so what?

I decided not to inquire whether there might be something else she had her eye on. Instead, I said, "Remember when we took that ferry to Center Island? It was fun."

"For little kids maybe."

"Well, where would you like to go?"

She had not left this afternoon's agenda to chance. "We have an assignment at school—report on the Ontario Science Center."

"All right, I'll take you there."

She wasn't much more talkative during the drive than she'd been before, but now it wasn't a surly silence; I figured she was dreaming of herself on rollerblades.

Before we entered the museum Paula requested a notebook and pen from her bag in the trunk.

They were having a special exhibition on bread. First, the biology of it: the molecular and chemical structures of wheat; also how it grows and reproduces. Then the agronomy: how it is farmed. The history of its use over the ages. What goes on in a gristmill. How, ultimately, the flour is shaped into loaves, how fermentation causes it to rise, how it is baked. The displays were beautifully mounted. Paula took notes. Peering through her glasses, writing down what she saw, she was beguiling.

At one point she found herself standing alongside a boy she knew. Attractive kid, red hair, athletic build—there with his father. She blushed saying hello. So did he. I expected her to move away from him as fast as she could, to avoid having to account for me. To my surprise, she said, "Meet my father. He flew up from New York to see me." There were handshakes; then we went our separate ways, my chest out a couple of inches.

There was something else she had to look at. When we got to the big glassed-in diorama I was immediately captivated. It was a re-creation of the fishing port of Osaka in an earlier time, peopled by miniature humans and animals (stationary but lifelike) going about their business. As we watched, the scene went through a telescoped twenty-four-hour cycle, from sunrise to dusk to lamplight, and later, the lamps extinguished, starry night.

I could tell that Paula was as charmed as I was.

It was almost four-thirty when we were ready to leave. We sat down on a bench in the hall to plot our next steps. Was there, I asked, a movie she'd like to see? She promptly named one, something with Bruce Willis. She knew where it was playing and the times it went on.

"It's too early for dinner and too late to do anything else," I said, "and the movie's almost an hour off. How about we have some ice cream, then go see the picture and save dinner till afterwards?"

"Okay." I could tell she was tired, and the good will I had bought seemed to be evaporating. The ice cream perked her up some, but not for long.

On the way to the theater I was asking myself Why is everything so goddamn hard?

Bruce Willis and his derring-do proved not to be my cup of tea, but it got us through the next couple of hours.

For dinner I suggested le Trou Normand, which I remembered agreeably. It was over the soup course that I said something that turned out to be inspired. "I had a good time at the Science Center. How about you?"

She acknowledged that it was interesting.

"If you liked that," I went on, "I think you'd enjoy going through the Krinsky Research Center. That's where I work." In case Mom hadn't mentioned it.

"You do research?" she asked.

"No, public relations. That means getting the center into the papers and on television when the scientists discover something. Like a new treatment for cancer.—And keeping it out of the papers and off the air if there are things we'd rather not talk about."

"What kind of things?"

"Well, at the moment we have one scientist dead under mysterious circumstances and another who's disappeared. A man and a woman."

"You think maybe somebody killed them?" I had her total attention now.

"We don't know what to think. I'm working with the police, looking for clues."

"*You're* doing that?"

"Yes."

"Like a detective!"

"I guess you could say."

"Wait till I tell Carol! And that gorpy Peter who's always talking about his father's private jet!"

I had suddenly become someone of consequence. She was looking at me in a whole different way.

"You've got suspects?"

"Some. A number of people could have a motive."

"Just like on TV!"

I drove home my advantage. "Maybe you'll come down some day and stay with me a couple of nights—over one of your holidays. I'll take you to the center and let people explain what they're doing. It's really interesting."

"Maybe I'll find a clue everybody else has missed!"

"Maybe you will. We could take in a Broadway show. Music . . . dancing."

"That'd be super!"

"If your mother would put you on a plane."

"I'll make her!"

Maybe yes, maybe no. But whatever might happen regarding a trip to New York, I'd broken through a barrier.

"Better finish your soup before it gets cold," I said. She set to with enthusiasm.

I suddenly saw myself introducing Paula and Eve to each other. Where had that picture come from? I must have been planning to see Eve again . . . and not just for help in trapping a killer, or killers.

I'd have to do something about that when I got back to N.Y. For now, I reached a decision. When I dropped Paula off at home I was not going to suggest picking her up for Sunday breakfast. Tonight we were buddies and I didn't see that my hanging around was going to improve anything. I'd tell her I'd had a wonderful time today and hoped she had too, but I had some work I had to get back to. Something highly secret. I'd promise to call her mother soon to try to schedule that visit.

Quit while you're ahead.

TEN

A new Almodóvar film was in town. Monday morning I rang Eve's extension and asked if she'd like to go see it with me tomorrow. As I was shortly to learn, I couldn't have come up with a better idea for a first date; Eve was a passionate movie buff. I offered her the choice of dinner before or after the show. She opted for after.

"That'll give us a chance to discuss the picture," she said—and added with what sounded like relish, "The worst fights I've ever had have been over movies!" Then while I was absorbing that: "How's your investigation going?"

"I wish I knew. I promise not to talk about it."

Monday afternoon, up on Fumi's floor, I ran into her in the hall. She looked and sounded as though she'd been through something. I asked how she was.

"All right, now. But Krinsky almost lost another one."

"What do you mean?"

"Saturday night I was on my way home from the video store. Just as I was passing the house next to mine a big piece of cornice fell off and landed on the sidewalk a foot away."

"Jesus!"

"If I'd been hit it would have killed me!"

"That's terrible! Is it an old house—in bad shape?"

"Maybe ninety—hundred years old. A brownstone. It looks all right from the outside."

"Places like that ought to be checked every so often. Did you call the police?"

"Yes, they came right away. The man who owns the house said he goes over it every spring and fall. He didn't find any cracks last time . . . nothing was loose."

"Most brownstones are set back from the sidewalk. Something just dropping off would land on the front steps or in an areaway.

"No, this one was built close up."

"Are you sure . . . were the cops sure . . . it wasn't someone trying to get you?"

"After a while I started wondering. I called the station—I talked to one of the men who'd come over. He'd been up on the roof, looked around. He said it was always possible some crazy had broken the piece off and thrown it, but that didn't mean I'd been picked for a special reason. He mentioned something like that going on around Times Square a while back. . . . masonry dropped from buildings. No one got hurt."

"I remember. Showtime . . . the side streets where the theaters are . . . Don't think they ever caught the guy. You tell him what's been happening at Krinsky . . . Faith and Dixon?"

"Yes, he said he'd check and see if there seemed to be any connection between them and me. Said it was natural to get upset, lady. Accidents do happen. I don't think he thought he was going to find anything."

"Well, maybe there's nothing to it. But until we know, you need some kind of protection."

She shook her head. "The police aren't going to provide it. And I refuse to go through each day worrying. I can't see why anyone would want to get rid of me anyway—unless it's some lunatic trying to depopulate the center." She turned to continue down the hall.

I held her a minute longer. "Could it have something to do with your going with me to Roosevelt Island? The possibility that we might have picked up a clue?"

She shrugged. "If it does have, then *you'd* better watch out."

Once Eve and I were settled at our restaurant table we started on a conversation that sped along the tracks like an A train between Columbus Circle and 125th Street. Fortunately, Almodóvar gave us nothing to fight over. Although the picture wasn't entirely believable, we'd both enjoyed it. It was alive, it was funny, we liked the postery bright colors.

Eve had grown up in a family—Brooklyn, Hasidic—where movies were regarded as sinful. From the age of nine she saw them on the sly. Her three-year-older brother, at sixteen, spotted her coming out of the theater playing, ironically, a picture with her name attached to it—*Three Faces of Eve*. (She was only being two-faced.) He threw a fit. What was she doing, watching such filth? "How do you know it's filth?" she shot back. "You've never been to the movies! *Three Faces of Eve* is wonderful!"

On the way home Avram extracted her defiant confession that she'd been spending allowances and lunch money on Hollywood's evil product for years. When they stormed into the house and Eve slammed into her bedroom, their mother didn't have to exert much pressure to get her son to tell all. Shocked, she ordered Eve out to face a verbal assault. A disgrace to her people and her God, she was forbidden ever to see another picture. Above all, any hint of her transgression must be kept from her father, who would suffer a stroke or heart attack if he so much as suspected.

I interrupted her story. "Why would your parents have named you Eve? Religious people . . . they must have believed Eve caused the downfall of the human race. Did they have something against you at birth?"

She smiled. "I'm sure they didn't think of it that way. Eve comes from 'hawwah'—means life in Hebrew."

It was the movie episode that convinced Eve she wasn't cut out to be a Hasid. As soon as she could she would break away from her family.—And remain forever a movie fan.

In order to have a roof over her head till she finished high school, she continued to live at home. Once she had her diploma, however, she got a job as a bank teller in Flatbush and moved into her own small apartment. Setting herself a rigorous schedule, she registered for night classes at Baruch College of the City University of New York in Manhattan, taking business courses and eventually graduating with honors. Meanwhile she'd been promoted several times at the bank, but quit banking to become bookkeeper for a construction company in Queens. With what she learned there, she qualified for a better-paying position—back again in Manhattan—with an engineering firm. She married one of the engineers, had a baby, stayed home. The boy grew up. He was now a sophomore on partial scholarship at the University of

Wisconsin. Eve's husband had died seven years ago, but before that she'd returned to work. This was her fifth year at Krinsky.

As good a listener as a talker, Eve had me opening memory closets full of stash I'd forgotten about. The words poured out like waters undammed as I recalled growing up in blue-collar Somerville, Mass., attending Boston University as a biology major, writing for the campus paper, then lucking into a reporter's job on the *Boston Globe*. Doreen was down from Toronto with a dance troupe when I met her. I'd just broken up with another girl (slender, fair), and Doreen (sturdy, brunette) was sufficiently unlike her to promise happier times. And we were happy, for a while. When Doreen's Boston prospects gave out and ambition dictated that she go to New York, I decided I didn't want to lose her. She went on ahead and after four months taking turns commuting to each other's pad, I was hired by the *New York Record*.

I told Eve about Doreen getting pregnant, which signaled her acceptance of the fact that she was never going to be a star ballerina. Then there was that novel I tried to write, which was supposed to make us rich and famous. It was based on a horrendous case I'd covered in Boston involving a little girl beaten to death by her mother's boyfriend.

"Somehow I could never get it down on paper," I said.

"Was that when Doreen was pregnant?"

"Yes. So I was under extra pressure to finish the book: we were going to need more money and a bigger apartment."

"Well, wouldn't that have been especially hard? I mean writing about a child being killed just when you were expecting one of your own?"

She was right, of course.

And I understood something else. "Yes. And I chose that subject because I really wasn't sure I wanted a baby. I didn't feel like a father. Until I held Paula in my arms."

"Sounds like my husband with Bobby."

I don't remember everything we said, or what we ate. All I know is we sat there a long time.

The restaurant was near the movie house showing the Almodóvar—Broadway across from Lincoln Center. Eve lived in Tudor City at the eastern end of Forty-first Street. I wanted to take her home by cab but she insisted on going alone on the bus; the 104 would drop her practically at her door. "If I had to be escorted home every time I went out at night," she said, "I'd never go anywhere. You can wait with me till the bus comes."

I saw her aboard, then sauntered down toward Fiftieth Street and my own crosstown bus, whistling as I went.

The next afternoon Eve called me to thank me for last night.

I asked if she'd be free to go out to dinner over the weekend.

"If it could be Saturday."

"You're on. Pick your favorite place."

"Have you been to Feltrinelli?"

"No, where is it?"

"East Forty-ninth. Nice, Northern Italian. Close to home for both of us."

"Sounds perfect. I'll reserve . . . what time?"

"How about eight, and come to my place first for a drink?"

She gave me her address and checked her Rolodex for Feltrinelli's number.

Tonight I had a date with Randi. I had to admit that as my interest in Eve grew my early excitement about Randi was waning. And I felt that some of the thrill had gone out of the relationship for her too. When you got right down to it, we didn't have a lot going between us except sex.

So that was what we concentrated on once again. It was not as great as at first . . . no surprises . . . but still pretty good.

As usual, we went our separate ways in the morning.

Coming home that evening, I picked up the mail in the lobby. When I sorted through it, my eye was caught by an envelope with my name and address crudely printed in pencil. It looked like something from a child. I opened it first. On a sheet torn from a tablet, also printed, was the following:

IF YOU WANT TO STAY ALIVE YOULL STOP MESSING AROUND

That was all.

It was enough to send a shiver along my spine.

I immediately thought of Fumi's narrow escape. In the

next second I felt Clyde's grip on my shoulder, then the punch in the face, as Randi and I left her place after our first night together,

Was this a warning from Clyde, or from someone who wanted me to stop playing detective? The same person or persons who might have tried to kill Fumi? If Clyde, how did he know my name and address? . . . Then I remembered giving Randi my card that morning.

Randi had assured me as recently as last week that Clyde was completely out of her life, but maybe she was lying and he'd seen the card.

I came to two conclusions: (1) Now that I knew Eve, I was ready to let Randi go. (2) If someone was trying to scare me into abandoning my hunt for a killer or killers, that must mean I was getting uncomfortably close. I might be scared— I definitely was—but this was no time to give up.

The first thing that struck me when I walked into Eve's apartment was that the foyer was a funny place to keep a bicycle. A purple bicycle at that.

She caught my look. "It's the only parking space I have."

"A beauty," I said. Which it was. Sleek . . . like a piece of strong but light sculpture against the wall. "Do you ride it a lot?"

"To and from work in nice weather. And I belong to a club . . . Pedal Pushers."

"Full of surprises." I followed her into the living room. The furnishings were untrendy and looked like they'd been around for a while. A fireplace, darkened with use. Mullioned windows (Tudor City was called that for a reason). In front of them a couple of spectacular avocados grown, no doubt from pits, occupying large oriental jardinières and reaching almost to the ceiling. Books out on the tables, jacket flaps tucked in where she'd left off reading. Apart from that an absence of clutter.

The liquor was in a small bowfront cabinet. Most people don't stock Irish whiskey, and Eve was no exception, but she *could* offer Glenfidet. I poured my own and added ice from a silver bucket while she went into the kitchen where she kept Finlandia in the freezer. Returning with her vodka on the rocks, she directed me to an upholstered armchair, man-sized, with matching footstool. "Try that—I think you'll find it comfortable." I guessed it had been her husband's. It *was* comfortable.

Sitting across from me on the sofa, she said, "I should have made dinner for you tonight. Next time I will."

"I accept. Do you like to cook?"

"I'm out of the habit. Used to. Oh, I still have friends in and I try to give them a decent meal, but cooking for one . . . Do you cook?"

"Fits and starts. I get tired of frozen dinners, and some-times I can't face eating out alone."

I brought up Pedal Pushers. A club, she'd said.

"Yes. We go on one-day jaunts. Tomorrow, Long Island . . . Jacob Riis Park."

"Isn't that pretty far?"

She nodded. "But manageable if you're in condition. I'd rather get my exercise biking than in some dumb class where you go through the same motions over and over."

"That can't be an ordinary bike."

"A Bianchi."

Never heard of it. "Ten speed?"

That showed how little I knew. "Twenty-one," she said. "Halfway between a mountain and a touring bike."

"I didn't know there *were* that many speeds."

"I don't use them all all the time." She laughed and changed the subject. "You didn't want to talk about The Mysteries of Krinsky the other night."

"Didn't want to bore you."

"I wouldn't be bored."

"Do you know Fumi Tashamira?"

"I know who she is."

"Friend of Frawley's. She went with me to Faith's apartment the first time I was there looking for clues. Then later she helped clear the place out. Last Saturday she was walking along the street near where she lives and a piece of cornice fell off a brownstone and just missed her. Fell off—or was thrown."

"You think someone was trying to kill her?"

"It's a possibility. The owner of the building said he inspected it twice a year and hadn't seen anything loose."

"Were the police . . . ?"

"Yes. Not much help there."

I told Eve what Fumi had reported after Faith's possessions were carted off—suitcases and casseroles missing but almost no clothes taken when she disappeared. I didn't mention the warning I'd received in the mail. That would have entailed explaining about Randi and Clyde—something I saw no need to go into with a woman I was beginning to hope would be Randi's successor, and then some.

Lacking any knowledge of the Randi situation, Eve tended to assume that if the cornice signified anything beyond a freak accident, it would have to be an attempt on Fumi's life. Being a realist, she said, "I don't suppose she can count on police protection?"

I shook my head. "They wouldn't be able to afford the manpower. Anyway, they'd need more proof of someone being out to get somebody."

"I hope that young woman can take care of herself," said Eve. "I hope you can too."

ELEVEN

Feltrinelli was one of those places where the lighting had a pinkish tinge, flattering to all. There were unobtrusive murals, not bad, of formal gardens, piazzas and ruins. Although quite full, the room was blessedly quiet. Ever since I'd researched an article on noise pollution and learned that some restaurants deliberately maintain a high decibel level—the sound of success, presumably—I'd lost patience with dining rooms where you couldn't hear yourself think. Tonight I was looking forward to more conversation without distraction.

Over our drinks we studied the menu; then, after the waiter had reeled off the inevitable specials, we ordered what we had decided on in the first place.

Eve had a glow about her not entirely attributable to the pink ambiance. She was wearing a beige two-piece linen outfit, a gold filigree chain and gold clip-on shell earings. Though hers was not a fashionable figure, she knew how to dress it with style. Her nails, not too long, sported a rosy finish. There was a touch of blue at the eyelids. I felt she had taken special pains with her appearance, and appreciated it. I was turned out in my olive drab tropical suit, brightened with a multicolored silk necktie in a free-form pattern, plus a peek of pocket handkerchief. Yesterday I'd had my hair cut and late this afternoon I'd given myself a second going-over of the day with my electric razor. We made a handsome couple.

I was thinking about Paula, indulging in a fantasy of her and Eve getting to know each other, when Eve asked, "How's your daughter?"

"Fine, I saw her over the weekend."

"Do you do that often?"

"Not often enough. But she doesn't make it easy for me. This time she wasn't too friendly starting out, then I happened to mention Frawley and Dixon and how I was involved. Suddenly I was daddy the detective. She liked that."

"She's how old?"

"Eleven."

"Siding with her mother?"

"Against me? Yes."

"I know it sounds trite, but some day when she's older she may start seeing your side of things."

"That's what I tell myself."

I knew very little about Eve's son, so I asked what Bobby was studying in college.

"Oh, he's not Bobby any more—now it's Robert." She was about to answer my question when my attention was diverted by the arrival of a young couple being shown to the table next to the one on my right. Her glance followed mine. The man was Gordon Barnard. I didn't recognize his date. Busy being seated, they didn't notice us.

I said in a low voice, "You know Gordon Barnard, from Dr. Wells' lab?"

"Yes. And Constance Stokes. But I don't think they'd remember me."

"She's very pretty. Wouldn't be the daughter of . . . ?"

"She would. T. Graydon's only child."

Gordon was looking around now, to check out his neighbors. He was surprised to find me two tables away. We said hello.

I turned back to Eve. "Flying rather high, isn't he?"

"Well, he's very presentable and they do say he has a future."

"But at this point kind of low on the totem pole. How would they have got together?"

"Could have been at the staff Christmas party—her father hosts it every year. They were both at the last one; she was standing in for her mother. Poor woman died a few months before."

Feltrinelli was not exorbitantly expensive, but Gordon couldn't be earning much; if he took Ms. Stokes often to places like this, I'd have thought it would strain his budget. Perhaps *she* bought the dinners. Well, it wasn't my problem.

We picked up where we'd left off about Robert and his course of study. He was majoring in physics but wasn't sure he wanted to make a career of it. For the last six months he'd been living with a girl, a fellow student. Eve hadn't met LouAnne but they'd talked on the phone and she sounded nice.

The waiter came to take Constance and Gordon's drink orders. I heard Constance say, "A glass of white wine."

"Very good, *signorina*. And you, *signore?*"

"Irish whiskey for me, on the rocks." Ah, a kindred spirit. As the waiter was turning away, Gordon said, "I don't suppose you have Tullamore Dew?"

"I'll check, sir, but I don't think so."

"Whatever you've got's okay."

My scalp prickled. . . . Was Gordon Barnard the visitor for whom Faith kept the single bottle of liquor? They were that friendly? Perhaps more than friendly? And if so, keeping their relationship secret?

"Would you say he's very ambitious?" I asked.

"Robert? Well, I think he will be when he knows what—"

"Not your son. I meant . . ." I inclined my head toward Barnard.

"Oh, that one. I don't really know him, but research is such a cutthroat business . . . You have to be ambitious to get anywhere."

The two of them were now staring into each other's eyes, rapt.

I couldn't stop talking about them. "They look serious. I wonder if her father knows."

"I'm told me he looks kindly on the young man. They've had him to dinner."

"You don't miss much, do you?"

"I try not to, in the interests of self-preservation."

If brains can spin, mine was setting a record for rpm's. Tullamore Dew didn't necessarily mean anything; it may have just been a coincidence. But if it wasn't? And if Gordon really was part of Faith's personal as well as professional life?

Fumi had said Faith was planning a showdown with her

boyfriend—fed up with the way he was treating her. Afterward she would tell Fumi who it was and what it was all about. Assuming the boyfriend had been Gordon and Faith knew he was dating Constance . . . I could see that with Constance being the big chief's daughter, it could give Gordon's career a considerable boost if he wangled his way into the Stokes family. Good reason for Faith to go on the warpath.

And if he ditched her, would she be willing to leave it at that? Or might she strike back—do something to spoil his game, prevent him from getting a foothold on the ladder?

If Gordon saw that coming, how far would he go to stop her?

Let's say the answer was he did kill Faith Frawley. How did that tie in with the death of Morgan Dixon? I now knew Dixon's and Wells's laboratories were competing for the same Staley funds, and I felt more than ever that the two mysteries were connected. But it was hard to believe that Gordon was so reckless of consequences that, having committed one murder in a situation where perhaps he could see no other way out, he would follow it with another under less pressing circumstances. Yet . . . why not? If his career was so important to him that he would kill once, mightn't he again? Maybe he was a sociopath and snuffing out a life didn't bother him. Maybe, getting rid of Faith, he'd found he enjoyed it. Maybe she hadn't been the first one.

Now that this whole new area of suspicion had opened, I'd have to figure out where to look for the relevant evidence. How to begin?

I became aware of Eve staring at me. Our appetizers had been served and she was half finished with hers; mine sat before me untouched.

"What is it?" she said.

"Sorry." I picked up my fork.

Until the main course was in front of us we kept up a conversation of some sort. Try as I might, however, I couldn't turn off the mental treadmill that had been set in motion. Nor could I stop stealing glances at the couple two tables away, who were too immersed in each other to notice. But Eve did. Finally, she said, with a touch of impatience, "I seem to have lost you."

It would have been silly to say "sorry" again, so I forbore. I made another effort at normal table talk, but wasn't very successful. If I could have told Eve what was running through my head, things might have been different. This time, though, I was reluctant to confide; my current scenario of evil-doing was built on such a flimsy foundation, it was as though I was afraid of having it knocked down by a breath of rationality. The mere fact that Barnard preferred a certain brand of whiskey was hardly damning; with no more than that to back it up I didn't feel justified in even hinting that he might be a murderer. For one thing, Eve's opinion of him could have an effect on his future at Krinsky. It wouldn't be fair to color it with my doubts. Not at this early stage.

Before dinner was over, I knew that tonight was not destined to be the night it might have been. Perhaps Eve would have been ready for me to try to advance our relationship to a more intimate stage, but my heart was no longer in it. My head, too, was elsewhere.

Whatever Eve had or had not been anticipating, she obviously sensed the change.

We skipped dessert and decided against espresso.

Gordon and Constance were twining fingers as we passed them on our way out.

Eve let me walk her home. She didn't ask me in. With a sudden rush of warmth toward her and regret for wasted opportunity, I was tempted to kiss her good night, but only took her hand for a moment. After watching her safely into the lobby, I started walking again.

My brain continued to stew with the questions and speculations that I couldn't let be. All the way home . . . over and over. They didn't stop when I got into bed. Around two o'clock I took a sleeping pill.

TWELVE

Sunday at three I phoned Randi. She answered in a guarded voice.

"Randi, I've got to ask you something."

"Yes?"

"Please level with me—it could be important. Have you been seeing Clyde?"

There was a pause. "Why do you ask?"

I was in no mood for games. "I'll tell you after you give me a straight answer."

"Well . . ." Dropping to almost a whisper: "He did want to talk to me . . . try to clear things up. He wasn't threatening or anything—I didn't feel I could refuse."

"Thanks. Has he been to your apartment?"

"I don't see what that has—"

"Has he?"

"Yes—once. So what?"

In the background I heard something . . . a voice, then music, as of channels being switched. Then another voice, maybe Randi's, making a shushing sound.

"He might not have threatened you," I said, "but someone's been threatening me."

"Someone . . . you don't know who?"

"No, but I think it'd be better if we don't see each other for a while."

Again a pause. "Well, if that's how you want it."

Did I detect a note of relief?

"It is. Thanks for all the fun. Stay well."

Gordon and Constance's dinner at Feltrinelli had been more meaningful than we knew. It was a celebration. When I arrived at my office Monday morning Altagracia, on the phone, said, "Just a minute, he's just walked in." Then, to me: "It's Ms. Claflin."

I slipped into my desk chair. "Hi, sweetheart. What's up?"

"Just wanted you to have some nice news for a change," said Hazel, "—instead of deaths and disappearances. Gordon Barnard and Stokes's daughter Connie are planning to get married. Soon."

For a minute I couldn't speak. *Nice* news? If Barnard was the person I suspected he was . . . Finally I found my voice: "*That's* a bombshell. Wow! I saw them having dinner together Saturday . . . holding hands."

"You do get around." I realized she thought "That's a bombshell" was sarcasm. This hot news, I seemed to be saying, was no surprise to me.

"Don't get me wrong," I said, "I'm fascinated. I wasn't sure how far it had gone."

"Where was this tête-à-tête Saturday?"

"Place called Feltrinelli."

"Don't know it."

"East Forty-ninth. Who gave you the scoop?"

"Stokes's secretary. He told *her* a few minutes ago. Happy about the whole thing. Thinks Barnard is a comer."

"That seems to be the general impression. He was Faith's teammate, you know."

"Yes. They must have been doing good work."

"Marrying Miss Stokes can't hurt his career. How are you fixed for a drink after work?"

"I can't. I got a call last night—Jane's in the hospital again. I'm going up there this afternoon for a couple of days."

"Sorry." I knew her sister in New Haven had health problems. "Good luck and thanks for the flash."

I was sorry not to have a chance to get Hazel's reaction to my dark misgivings. We'd been buddies so long that I felt free to share with her what I'd withheld from Eve.

That afternoon, caught up with my work, I leaned back in my swivel chair and asked myself what I should do next. There had to be a way for me to get at the truth about Gordon and Faith. I was sure that if Hazel and I could hash over the problem, she'd come up with an idea.

But Hazel wasn't available . . . and Eve was.

Teetering in my chair, I told myself I was being unfair to Eve. I'd decided practically as soon as we'd met that she was trustworthy, yet at the first significant test I had chosen not to confide in her all the way. Also I was convinced of her intelligence, astuteness and practicality—qualities that could make her really useful in helping me plan a strategy.

So why wasn't I in her office now, or down in the cafeteria with her, taking her into my confidence and asking for suggestions? The roadblock still in place was my reluctance to prejudice her against someone she might be in a position to harm and who, when all the facts were known, might turn out to be innocent.

On the other hand . . . Hazel had said Gordon and Connie were planning to marry *soon*. That didn't allow much time for ethical shillyshallying.

What the hell. I picked up the phone and punched Eve's extension.

I'd concluded that the cafeteria was safer than her office; no danger of being overheard. So here we were, sitting across from each other with coffee and muffins.

"I know you knew that something had come over me the other night," I said, "in the restaurant."

She nodded.

I proceeded to explain . . . about my overhearing "Tullamore Dew," and the ugly questions it had raised.

Eve listened gravely as I formulated the questions: Had Barnard been Faith's lover? Had he abandoned her for Constance? Had he killed Faith—or, another possibility that hadn't occurred to me till now, had she gone off somewhere, crushed, to be alone . . . or perhaps to take her own life?

I wound up with the latest worrisome development: the impending marriage.

What was to be done? Was there anything I'd overlooked—any path still untaken—in my efforts to find out more than the little I knew?

Eve broke off a piece of muffin but forgot to eat it. After a moment she spoke: "It seems to me there's just one area you're sure of where Faith and Barnard have been involved together—their research. The rest is all maybe. I don't sup-

101

pose there could be a clue in what they were doing as a team."
She shook her head, rejecting her idea. "No, that doesn't
make sense."

I was ready to agree with her, disappointed that this was
the best she could come up with. Then I started thinking
about it. Those papers I'd been given describing their work
. . . I'd barely glanced at them, searching for points of simi-
larity to investigations going on in Dixon's lab. I hadn't found
any, and also I hadn't understood a lot of what I was reading.
Maybe I *should* take another look, even though I couldn't
imagine what kind of a lead I might pick up in grant applications or research reports.

"It may make sense," I said, "—looking at the research.
I've done it once but not carefully."

"It'll probably be a waste of time."

"Who knows?"

I still had the kit with the material on Faith and Gordon's
collaboration assembled for me by Wells's secretary. It included a preprint of their *Cell* paper, which had since come
out in the scheduled issue. (Wells was listed as coauthor
though he probably hadn't contributed anything—common
practice in the society ruled by chiefs of laboratories.) I
started by reading that article as the latest, most up-to-date
statement.

It was hard going, requiring frequent recourse to the medical dictionaries and science books I'd been accumulating. I
had to pick my way through every paragraph at least twice.
As I'd gathered my first time around, Gordon and Faith were
focusing on oncogenes, DNA sequences that cause normal
cells to turn cancerous. They were hoping to stimulate macrophages to produce anti-oncogenes which could attack
the oncogenes. These they would clone and insert into cancer cells, rendering them inoperative. Macrophages? Scav-
enger cells circulating through the bloodstream, destroying
invaders.

One could assume that macrophages contained anti-
oncogenes because macrophages so rarely became cancerous.
There were many types of anti-oncogenes in existence, probably between fifty and a hundred.

Frawley and Barnard (and, nominally, Wells) had been performing a series of experiments, the first of which consisted of taking normal cells in tissue culture and transfecting them with a standard oncogene. This had converted the normal cells to proliferating cancer cells. The next step, as reported in *Cell*, had been to transfect the resulting cancerous cells with a newly-created anti-oncogene, restoring them to normalcy.

So far everything was being done in vitro. The goal, of course, was to put the findings to clinical use.

Weary from my intense concentration, I was doggedly persisting in reading on to the end where the experiments that still lay ahead were described. The next thing I knew I'd dozed off and my forehead hit the desk. I recovered with a start, sitting up sharply. It hadn't been much of a bang, but it may have shaken up some neurons and created new pathways of association, because suddenly I was thinking "oncogene . . . uncogene . . . Uncle Gene . . ."

Was that too big a stretch? . . . If you were hearing it through a wall and not able to make out the context?

"Your fucking Uncle Gene's—I'll make sure everybody knows!" The neighbor, Maria Marinello, had said it was something like that. A woman's voice—sounded like Faith. And a man . . .

Could two members of the human race really get into a deadly fight over some ticky-tacky speck of DNA? Why not— if, for instance, there was something phony about the research, some falsification of the findings? . . . And if Gordon had just told her their affair was finished and she was striking back by threatening to expose the fraud?

It would have hurt her too, of course—unless she could pin all the blame on him. But even if she couldn't, bringing him crashing down might have been worth it to her even if they came crashing together.

There'd been a number of instances in recent years of scientists fudging or faking results. One researcher had gone so far as to paint black spots on white mice to prove a point. Another published the "findings" of a diet study on children with elevated cholesterol levels, and doctors were prescribing on the basis of his research—until it turned out there was nothing to back it up. The president of The Rockefeller University had had to step down after strenuously defending a dishonest published report by an associate—a report he had endorsed. If an individual at that level could practice or abet deceit, it wasn't too hard to believe that someone on the way up might play footsy with the facts.

I'd written about several of those cases for *Inside Story* and knew there had to be many more that never got exposed.

I was getting excited and felt confined in my cubicle. What I needed was to get out and take a walk. There'd been a break in temperature and humidity; fresh air might restore order to my mind in which wild conjecture was probably running roughshod over common sense.

My watch showed that it was almost the end of the working day anyway. I'd walk home—something I often considered doing but, in sticky summer weather, rarely did. Wrapped up in my wild speculations, I nevertheless remembered to observe the new rule I'd set for myself—to walk as close to the curb as possible, in case anyone was planning to drop something from a roof or a window.

It crossed my mind to call Eve and tell her that her suggestion, which she'd stopped short of actually making, looked like it might pay off. But not yet. I hadn't thought things through as far as I needed to. Even if I was on the right track, which was far from certain, there was still a lot left unexplained.

Maybe when I stopped pumping adrenalin so hard, the scenario I'd been spinning about Gordon and Faith and oncogenes would resemble one of those great ideas you have in the middle of the night.

You know the kind. Next morning, forget it.

THIRTEEN

I had one of those great ideas in the middle of the night, and the next morning it still looked great.

Great but terrible. I scarcely slept, and this time I didn't take a sleeping pill, because what I was thinking banished any desire to sleep; and if sleep were to come, I feared the dreams it might bring.

Daylight did nothing to improve my state of mind. It simply made my imaginings seem more real.

Maria Marinello had heard a man and a woman, presumably Faith, quarreling. Guy Brammell and his roommate, who occupied the apartment under Faith's, had heard something that sounded like a power tool. A drill or a saw, they thought. It had continued for maybe half an hour.

Let's start from the premise that Gordon was Faith's faithless lover and killed her when she threatened to blow the whistle about the faked oncogene research. He could have done it with a blow, or by strangulation, or by poison if perhaps he'd pretended to knuckle under and they'd made their peace and were drinking—he Tullamore Dew, she a Coke or tea or coffee. Who knows? The method of murder doesn't matter. It's what I visualized as following that gave me the shivers: the murderer dismembering the corpse with a saw, mopping up the blood with the missing towels Fumi had mentioned and stuffing the body parts into the two large suitcases, likewise missing. Suitcases weighted with the heavy Creuset casseroles and frog bookends, which also had vanished.

The obvious place to dispose of the suitcases would have been the East River . . . but there was a question as to how practical that would have been. I remembered seeing paved walks near the water's edge; they were railed in, and beyond the railings I had the impression there were rocks, some of them almost the size of small boulders. Could even a strong young man have heaved the suitcases over and out far enough to clear the rocks? And was there a secluded spot close enough to Faith's apartment so that he could have lugged his horrid luggage there and got rid of it without danger of being seen?

I dressed, shaved and gulped breakfast in a fever of impatience. As soon as possible I wanted to go out and renew my acquaintance with the island, this time concentrating on the topography.

Now that my scenario had survived the night and even developed added features, Eve had to be clued in. My hope was that she would be able to drop everything and take the tramway with me.

A little after nine I walked into her office, shut the door and set forth my whole reconstruction of events leading up to the tragedy, and beyond. When I got to the explanation of Uncle Gene, her eyes lit up and she brought her palms together miming applause. Eve was not easily flappable, but as I went on to the gruesome part I could see she was shaken. The color had drained from her face by the time I was finished.

We sat in silence for a few seconds. Then she asked, "How soon do you want to go?"

"As soon as you can be ready."

"Give me ten minutes."

When we touched down on the island and emerged from the shelter, we began heading in the same direction as our fellow passengers—to the right, where the apartment houses and stores were clustered. Before long, however, we veered off from the others, aiming for the paved walk along the water.

I soon confirmed that my hazy recollection had been correct: there were rocks beyond the railing, creating a considerable setback from the water. Eve agreed with me that anyone trying to throw heavily weighted suitcases into the river could hardly count on achieving a splash. Also, someone making the attempt, or even succeeding at it, would be visible to whoever might be looking out of an apartment window or sitting on a balcony. Would Gordon Barnard or anybody else acting with cool calculation be that foolhardy?

We had to admit that we doubted it.

Of course the suitcases could have been carried to some other part of the island . . . though not, we thought, very far. It occurred to me that I hadn't explored what lay just to the left of the exit from the tramway station. The distance there from Faith's building would probably have been manageable. We started back that way to take a look.

A few minutes later we were approaching the lofty bridge tower alongside which the tramway was suspended. Then we found ourselves beneath the span, traffic humming overhead. Just past the place where the tower was anchored to the earth, we turned right, down to the water's edge. The ground under our feet was stony, but we could walk quite close to the river. Getting rid of the suitcases here would not have been such a problem. Furthermore, once we had gone around the tower's massive base, we were no longer in plain sight of everybody who might happen to be glancing our way.

"This is where he did it!" I exulted to Eve.

"I think you're getting warm," she said, bringing me back to reality, reminding me that however convincing a hypothesis may be, in science or in life, it doesn't mean a thing without facts.

I thanked her for coming and saw her off in the next gondola, so she could get on with her day's work. I still had another place to go, having used the pay phone at the terminal and ascertained that Lieutenant Balch of the 114th Precinct would be able to see me.

While I was waiting for the bus to take me off the island to Queens, I realized something that hadn't occurred to me before: Barnard might have driven out here across the bridge *from* Queens, then back again with the butchered body. The East River wouldn't necessarily have been the only possible place to dump it.

The bus came. I boarded. Soon I was in the station house, less sure of certain details than I had been.

"How are those poor people?" Balch asked, motioning me to a chair and settling his ample flesh behind his desk.

"The Frawleys? Pretty much given up hope."

He plucked a lighted cigarette from his ashtray, took a drag, stumped it out. "You said you thought you were on to something."

"Yes, but nothing that points to Faith being alive. Just the opposite."

"Even proof that she's dead might be some relief to the parents."

"Well . . ." I hoped that my version of what had happened wouldn't fall flat on its face when tried out on a professional.

His face remained impasssive as I reported, first, what Fumi had said about a showdown with a mysterious boy-friend; what Faith's neighbors had heard and what Fumi had ticked off as missing from the apartment. I then proceeded to Dixon's death, which was news to him, and which I suggested might be related either to community hostility to the medical center's expansion, to competition for new lab space or funding, or to Faith's disappearance. I told him about Barnard and Constance Stokes and their plan to marry, and my hunch that Barnard was the boyfriend whose identity Faith had kept secret. The showdown could have been over his defection.

I hesitated and hemmed and hawed before finally daring to advance my Uncle Gene-oncogene theory—my biggest speculative leap—and watched for some glimmer of expression on his part that would tell me how that was going over. No reaction. I brought up the sound of the power tool again, suggesting that a saw had been used to dismember Faith's body after the man she'd been fighting with—Gordon Barnard—had killed her. Having just come from Roosevelt Island, I described how he could have disposed of the evidence in the East River, adding that of course he might have used a car to transport the remains elsewhere.

Winding down, I asked if I he thought I was right to think that if Barnard was capable of one murder, he might have got rid of his laboratory's competitor, Dr. Dixon. Then I sat back in my seat, sweating even though the air conditioning was on.

I realized that during my recital Balch, a chain smoker the other time I'd seen him, hadn't lit a cigarette. Mightn't that be a good sign?

It was. He said, "It's time we moved Faith Frawley from missing persons to homicide."

I let out a sigh, the breath I'd been holding back. "I'm not a nut case?"

He shook his head slowly side to side. "I don't know yet. You seem to make sense. This guy Barnard, he doesn't have any idea you suspect him?"

"I don't see how he could have."

"Good." He picked up his phone, punched an extension. "Balch here, sir. We've been following a missing persons case—now it looks like homicide. Can you see a Mr. Swain—I've got him with me now—he'll tell you about it? Okay, right away." He stood up. "Come with me."

As we walked across a hall he identified the man I was about to meet as Captain Fraker. "Just give him the story like you did me."

Captain Fraker was a tall man in good trim, going gray. He greeted me with a forceful handshake. Balch, curious I guess as to how my scenario would play to a new audience, stayed on after introducing us.

When the three of us were seated, Fraker asked me, "What exactly is your interest in this case?"

"It started as part of my job. I was hired as the new Director of Media Relations for the Krinsky Research Center in Manhattan. I hadn't been there very long when one of the research workers disappeared. The center had just had some unfavorable publicity, so I was asked to find out what I could—maybe there was a simple solution . . . Dr. Frawley might have walked off the job . . . something like that . . . and we wouldn't have to call the police. Well, finally we realized we did have to call the police"—I nodded toward Balch—"but I kept poking around anyway. By then I was feeling pretty sure something bad had happened to her, and now I think she was murdered and I know who did it. That is, I think I know who did it."

"Okay, I get the picture."

I repeated what I had just been over with Balch. When I

forgot to mention the frogs among the missing objects, he interrupted to remind me.

Fraker allowed himself to show interest along the way. A couple of times he asked a question, to clarify a point. At the end he said, "You make it sound plausible. I'll put a couple of men to work on it. Maybe you can help us a little further, if you would. How well do you know Barnard?"

"Not very. Just to the extent that we've been brought together by this case."

"Could you get a little more friendly? Over a drink? If you can, find out if he owns a car or knows somebody who might've lent him one. If not, we'll check rental places in his neighborhood to see if there's a record of his taking out a car that weekend. Try to lead the conversation to research fraud. . . . Power tools, does he do any carpentry? Whatever might give him away. Maybe if he had no idea what you were up to, he might even see no harm in admitting he was in the woman's apartment that night."

"I can try."

"Where does he live?"

"I don't know; I'll find out."

"I have a Manhattan phone book. Let's see if he's listed." Fraker located the page and ran his finger down. "Here he is on West Sixty-eighth." Setting the directory aside, he said, "I'll have the East River dragged at the spot where you think the suitcases might have gone in—and anywhere else that looks possible. I'll want you to meet with the detectives I'm assigning, but they're not around now. Could they come see you or do you want to come back here again tomorrow?"

"They could come to my office—or to my apartment before I leave for the office if that wouldn't be too early. It might be better if nobody at Krinsky sees them."

"Tell me where you live . . . what time."

I brought out a business card, turned it over and wrote my home address. "How's eight-thirty?" I said, handing it to Fraker.

"They'll be there. Their names are Holsclaw and Sanchez. And thanks."

"Thank *you*." Now it was in the pros' court. I felt as though a big load had lifted.

110

Back at work, I phoned Eve to bring her up to date. This was one of those times when both she and her secretary were away from their desks, so I left my name on the answering machine, and a few minutes later Eve called back.

"How did it go?"

"Very well. I think we may see some action."

"Good. How about tonight for that home-cooked meal?"

"Just because you said something in a reckless moment . . . I could pick you up and we'd go someplace."

"No, I want to."

"Then so do I."

I could remember the days when if you were looking to buy flowers in New York you found a florist, and those weren't on every other block. Now there are Korean markets everywhere you turn, each market with its outdoor array of tulips, roses, carnations and what have you, to say nothing of those boring house plants adapted to the city. The ones that can grow without sunlight—or sometimes even daylight. They ♡ New York. On the way from my place on Fifty-first to Eve's on Forty-first, I picked up a dozen roses in a sort of apricot color, pale at the base of the petals, a deeper shade at the tips. I thought the apricot would complement her own coloring; I hoped she wasn't an uncompromising red-roses girl. When we were growing up I understood those to represent a declaration of undying passion, and I didn't think we were far enough along for that.

She loved the roses. She'd started something in the oven and was a little flushed when she answered the door chime. The humidity had eased this evening, allowing her to turn off the air conditioning, which she confessed she didn't like. Warmth emanated from the kitchen. A strand of dark hair had come loose and curled over her forehead on which there were beads of perspiration. I liked the way she looked.

I accepted her suggestion to hang my jacket in the closet while she was arranging the roses in a vase. On top of the bowfront liquor cabinet stood a bottle bearing a familiar label: Bushmills. *Black* Bushmill at that, premium Irish. It hadn't been here last time.

111

"Fix yourself a drink," she said. She set the vase on a side table next to the sofa.

"You bought this specially for me." Bottle in hand, I crossed to her side and kissed her gently on the lips.

We held it a moment, then she drew away. "Enjoy it."

"I already am."

She laughed. "I'll be right back with my vodka."

"I don't believe in fancy hors d'oeuvres," she explained, returning with her drink in one hand and a plate in the other. On the plate were *crudités* and a tricolor vegetable paté . . . carrot, cauliflower and spinach, I was told. "Better than it looks." Another plate, with crackers, was on the coffee table, as were brightly decorated paper cocktail napkins.

"Now tell me what happened after I left you this morning. You went to see the detective in Queens. . . ."

I nodded. "He listened to everything I had to say and said it seemed to make sense."

"Good."

"So I said, 'Then you don't think I'm a nut case?' and he said, 'I don't know yet,' but he took me across the hall and introduced me to the captain in homicide, who also listened and said it all sounded plausible and he was going to put a team to work on it."

"That's wonderful. I'm proud of you."

"I'm kind of proud of myself. More surprised than anything . . . getting this far."

"Do they think Frawley and Dixon are connected?"

"I think they're willing to consider it."

She wanted to hear everything and I gave her a play-by-play account. I told her of Fraker's request that I buddy up to Barnard and try to get information out of him without his realizing it.

"Buddy up to Uncle Gene?" said Eve with a shudder. "I don't think I could bear to."

"We still might be wrong about Uncle Gene," I said. I didn't believe it.

"If I turn out to be wrong, I'll cook *him* a dinner. Him and his bride. Though why would they want to come?"

"She might like to get out of a night in the kitchen. Hey, I've thought of something else I ought to do—might help the detectives. I should talk to Dr. Wells, raise the question with him whether Gordon might have falsified the *Cell* report ... maybe with Faith's connivance. As though I'd just begun to get suspicious. He might have had his own suspicions ... kept them to himself."

"Yes, if he did, he might say something interesting ... unexpected."

I was suddenly tired. I realized it had been a day of tension.

Eve's radar seemed to pick it up. "Are you about ready to eat?"

"Mm. It smells wonderful."

A small table had been set up in the foyer. Linen cloth, elegant sterling, fine crystal, a cluster of daisies in a little bowl. Pausing on her way to the kitchen she handed me a matchbook. I lit the two candles in their cut glass holders.

We dined on roast chicken, with the trimmings and a California white wine that was dry but had body and *pétillement*. We talked, not about The Case, but about things we'd enjoyed in our lives ... in our very different pasts before we knew each other.

Things that we could now look forward to enjoying again together.

113

FOURTEEN

After dinner we left the dishes in the sink and got right down to lovemaking. First, standing in the kitchen doorway.

After a slow, exploratory embrace, mouth on mouth, legs pressing, fingers locking, we broke. She took my hand then and led me across the foyer into the bedroom. Without a word she drew down the bedspread, and after that, she on the far side of the bed, we untucked the light blanket and top sheet.

The air conditioner in one of these windows was on, at a medium setting. She asked, "Shall I turn this off?"

"It's a little cool, but why not leave it? We'll be generating heat."

She smiled. "I hope so."

A moment later we were out of our clothes, lying on the crisp bottom sheet.

We touched each other gently, carefully. Her skin had the texture of fine cloth. I felt my own flesh coarser under her fingers. Soon, comfortable with ourselves and each other, we roamed freely.

There's something to be said for middle-aged sex. The rockets going off don't have to be the most dazzling that ever spangled the heavens; if the earth shakes it doesn't have to bust the seismograph. Yes, there's a lot to be said for middle-aged sex, and that night we said it. And said it again.

Sanchez and Holsclaw arrived at my place at eight-thirty sharp. Their suits and shirts may have been fresh when they set out, but they were already beginning to wilt. The humidity was back. Both detectives had loosened their ties.

Sanchez was short, dark and muscular, his partner ruddy and inclined to beef. They turned down my offer of coffee or a cold drink. We sat in the living room with the venetian blinds tilted to dull the brightness and I went through my story for . . . what was it, counting Eve? . . . the fourth time in two days. I was getting rather good at it. After presenting all the facts as I understood them, I explained how I planned to buddy up to Barnard, if I could, in hopes of flushing out something more. They told me the river-dragging crew was supposed to start work this morning. They themselves seemed eager to be about their business and were on their feet and out in under twenty minutes.

Getting chummy with Barnard turned out not to be easy. Understandably for a man with a new fiancée, his time away from the lab was almost completely booked. When I suggested we have lunch or drinks together, he begged off; he was meeting Constance, they were going shopping for things they'd need. Though I would have preferred the relaxed atmosphere of a bar, I finally managed to lure him to the cafeteria one day in mid-afternoon. He seemed a little puzzled as to why I was so persistent.

"You're probably going to be off on your honeymoon pretty soon," I said as we sat down to our coffee and Danish. "Your *Cell* report may start attracting attention while you're gone. Maybe you'd want to leave me an itinerary, with phone numbers—or would you rather be left alone?"

He considered. "Well, I've had a few calls . . . people saying it sounded interesting. If there are a few more, I don't imagine it'd be anything that couldn't wait."

"In that case I'll just put them on hold."

"I think that'd be the best idea."

"Have you set a date yet?"

"Connie and her dad are working on it now. They want to keep it a small wedding . . . her mother having passed away last fall, they don't feel like splurging. Which is fine with me. So as soon as they can get all the right family members together, theirs and mine . . ."

"Within the next couple of weeks?"

"Something like that."

"Will you be driving off somewhere on your honeymoon? Do you have a car?"

It didn't sound to me like I was making normal conversation but he didn't seem to notice.

"As a matter of fact we *are* planning to drive through New England, but we'll have to rent a car. I couldn't afford to keep one in New York."

"And when you get back ... How are you around the house? Handy with tools?"

He looked a bit surprised; I felt the artificiality of my dialogue was beginning to strike him, but he answered, "Handy enough. I can slap together a bookcase. But then there's all that sanding and finishing. The hell with it."

I floundered on. "I think some guys really take to marriage because they can set up a workshop in the basement. Childhood dream for some of them.—Not that there's much chance of that if you live in Manhattan, unless you buy a house."

"A house? On our income? Even with Connie and me both working ..."

Trying to zero in on whether he owned a power saw, I could think of no way to ask naturally. Also I began to see danger in moving on to my next questions. To bring up the subject of research fraud, after having just mentioned the *Cell* article, would put him on guard if he had indeed been guilty of faking results. And so would any attempt to find out whether he had been to Faith's apartment *that* night, assuming he had been.

I wondered if there was a technique I didn't know for extracting information from the unwary.

The trouble was, Gordon Barnard was wary. That didn't prove guilt but it added to the difficulty of putting anything over on him. Our conversation wound down and neither of us made an effort to prolong it beyond the last of the pastry and coffee. When we parted, I congratulated him on his coming nuptials. I suspected he was asking himself what our little get-together had been about.

Now I would have liked to move on to the session I'd planned with Dr. Wells, where I'd bring up the subject of possible research fakery ... but alas, he was out of the country: conference in Scotland, and from there he was going to London.

116

My relationship with Eve had shifted to low gear. Not that we'd run into trouble. She had decided—no doubt sensibly—that we shouldn't rush things; we shouldn't expect to see each other every day or make sex a nightly routine. Habit, she said, is easier to get into than out of. Let's enjoy each other without swallowing each other up . . . see how it goes.

We talked on the phone before the weekend and I relayed the latest word from the police. A check of hardware stores and lumber outlets where Gordon might have rented a saw had produced nothing. Same with neighborhood auto rental stations. Dragging the East River also had proved fruitless. Seems that if weights had been employed, they might have been heavy enough to keep the suitcases down but not so heavy as to withstand the strait's powerful currents. There was no telling where Faith Frawley might have ended up, whether north of Roosevelt Island or south on the bottom of New York Bay.

Over the weekend Eve and I maintained our distance. Then on Tuesday I took her to dinner again and we went to bed again (at my place for variety) and it was as good as before—or better. After that we let a few days pass.

The next time, another homecooked meal at Eve's. Her mood was upbeat: she had just heard from her son that he and his girl would be coming to New York to visit friends next weekend. She'd be having dinner with Robert and Lou-Anne on Saturday and would love to have me join them. I was pleased to be invited.

The following Monday she'd be leaving for a conference in Atlanta—nonmedical health professionals—and from there would be off to visit her husband's relatives in Fort Worth, so Saturday would be my last chance to see her for more than a week.

The day came for Wells's return, a Wednesday, and after allowing him a another day's grace I requested a meeting. He wanted to put it off but I told his secretary it was important. He made time for me that afternoon, Thursday.

Something had bothered me about my original intention to tell Wells I'd grown suspicious of Barnard in connection with the *Cell* report. No scientist myself, on what grounds would I have challenged it? Why would I have been wonder-

ing about it in the first place? I certainly didn't want Wells
to get any hint that I suspected his trusted subordinate of
something else related to research fraud ... something
worse. This problem kept nagging at me until yesterday when
I suddenly saw—or thought I saw—how to get around it.
Now that I was on my way to Wells's lab I wished I'd talked
it over with Eve, but sometimes I felt I was laying too much
on her. After our first date, when Barnard had ordered Tullamore Dew and Eve had lost me, there'd been other moments when I sensed slight annoyance at my preoccupation
with what we now referred to routinely as The Case. Sometimes it did seem to loom too large—to relegate her to second
place in my concerns.

Now here I was walking into Wells's office, ready to employ
a tactic I'd discussed with no one.

As always when I saw him on his home turf, he was jacketless, open-collared. His glasses rested on their usual spot
halfway down his nose.

"Thanks for seeing me on such short notice," I began. "I
hope you had a good trip."

"You said it was urgent, I believe. Yes, fine."

Now that I had him waiting impatiently, my mouth went
dry. It was damned awkward to have to tell somebody that a
person employed by him in a responsible position might be
a liar. Even concealing my darker suspicion of murder, this
was a nasty moment. I reminded myself it was Wells who had
first turned me into a private eye, asking me to investigate
Frawley's disappearance. It wasn't my fault if the trail appeared to lead to his own lab.

"This is a little difficult," I said. "A very personal question:
did you ever really have time to go over that *Cell* piece—the
one with Frawley and Barnard—so that you were familiar
with every step of the experiment?"

I detected a slight tensing of his body. "Why do you ask?"

"I know how productive your lab is. And I also know that
the chief routinely puts his name on something to give it a
boost even if he may have been too busy to work on it." (And
to give himself a boost, I might have added.)

He waved the softsoap aside. "You must have a reason for
bringing up this particular report."

"Well, it's not my idea, but the police have a theory. They've heard about doctored research results and false claims like everyone else; it interests them . . . almost like a new category of crime. Anyway, they're wondering if maybe Faith Frawley reached a point where she wanted to be recognized for important work . . . where she'd be tempted to nudge the facts a little. They've formed a picture of her as a pretty determined woman. But they also see her as basically conscientious . . . honorable. They say to me, Could she have got cold feet when the paper was about to be published? Incidentally, they think that as senior investigator she probably got Barnard to go along with the deception—if there was one. Then the cold feet—and, according to the theory, she took a powder." I paused. "Does any of this make sense to you?"

He did not answer at once. Some of the tension seemed to ease out of him. Then he said quietly, "In a sorry sort of way . . . yes, it makes sense." He sighed. "And it would certainly be better if she'd decided to drop out of sight than if someone had killed her."

"I wonder . . ." I pressed my advantage. "I wonder if you'd care to talk to Barnard or review the workbooks for the experiment. If there's anything wrong we should find out now. It's especially delicate with him and Constance Stokes about to get married. It would look bad if—"

"Oh yes, yes. If it came out later. Of course." He stopped and reflected. "Today's Friday. Why don't I take those workbooks with me when I go to the country later today. Gordon's already left—he'll be with the Stokes in Greenwich for the weekend. I told him to leave early, but I know where the books are kept. And" . . . a sudden inspiration . . . "look, I've been wanting to invite you to our place, and this would be a good time. Come tomorrow, stay through Sunday—it'll give us a chance to settle this messy business." He shook his head. "I can't really believe either Faith or Gordon would go off the track like that."

"Thank you—I'd like to. But—"

Once before, he'd spoken of having me visit and had said something about my bringing a friend. Not this time. But then, Eve couldn't have made it anyway.

"There'll be a few other guests," he went on. "Cliff Harron and his wife. The Nortons—that's Emily Norton."

She was the one Hazel had suggested for Dr. Dixon's replacement as chair of the professional center staff fundraising committee. Harron was the chairman of the Krinsky center board of trustees. I'd been introduced to him once; here was a chance to become better acquainted.

I was torn. Saturday . . . the dinner with Eve's son; I'd promised to be there. But these next two days could be crucial. If Wells did discover fraud, I would hate not being around to see—and maybe help determine—what happened next. This was what all my efforts had been leading up to.

Yet, to disappoint Eve . . . And she might be more than disappointed—a little hurt as well. Still, it wasn't as if either of us had any real claim on the other. So far we were just friends, and casual bedmates. She'd made it clear she valued her independence.

Wells cut in on my thoughts. "Do you play tennis?"

"What?" It took me a second to refocus.

"Tennis. A neighbor has a court. We might drop over. And we have a swimming pool. If you want to bring a racket . . . trunks . . . Come prepared for a good time!"

I decided I had to go.

"I'll be happy to."

FIFTEEN

Back at my desk, I picked up the phone and punched the three digits of Eve's extension.

She was glad to hear from me, which made me feel guilty. Before I could state my business, she said, "I hope you like baked ham—it's Robert's favorite. With candied sweet potatoes."

"Ah . . . Eve. I'm sorry, but I . . ."

"You can't make it?"

"I just had a meeting with Dr. Wells. It's complicated and I'll explain later. He's taking Barnard and Frawley's workbooks to the country over the weekend, looking for fraud, and he wants me to be there. I put him up to it—this could be where we nail Barnard. I do want to meet Robert and I'm sorry—"

"Don't worry about it—you'll meet another time. I can't wait to hear what happens." She added, "Watch your rear!"

Wells had said someone would pick me up in Mt. Kisco, and when I stepped off the train early the next afternoon, there he was in person on the station platform. He was dressed in chino shorts and an unbuttoned shirt that revealed a mat of brown hair matching the curls on his head. Unlike his regular glasses, sunglasses sat well up on the nose where he could look through them—a concession, no doubt, to the demands of driving.

"I thought you'd send somebody else," I said as he led the way to his car, which turned out to be a Jeep. This wouldn't have been what he drove into Manhattan the night he got robbed; he'd spoken of the candlesticks being stolen out of the trunk. "I could have taken a taxi."

"No problem. Always glad for an excuse to get away from

the houseguests. Don't get me wrong, I like houseguests, but every so often I need a chance to recharge."

We hooked up our seatbelts and started moving. The day was hot, though a little less oppressively so than in the city.

I took a deep breath. Country air.

"Did you bring your swim trunks?"

"In my bag. And a tennis racket."

"Yes, I saw that."

I was burning to ask if he'd had a chance to look at the workbooks but felt he'd tell me when he was ready. So I made small talk. "Beautiful out here. Do you own much land?"

"Fifteen acres."

I was impressed. "Must keep you busy weekends."

"It does. But a lot of it's undeveloped. And I have help. And Jessica spends most of her time up here. She's a demon gardener."

We were putting the town behind us, climbing a hill. Soon we were on a curving road lined with stone fences beyond which were sweeps of lawn, shrubbery, ancient trees and expensive houses. After a while we turned off into another road; the houses grew farther apart, sometimes disappearing into protective greenery. At last Wells said, "Here we are," and swung into an opening between two fieldstone pillars topped by urns of impatiens and ivy.

His house, baronial, stood at the crest of a bluestone drive. A few magnificent trees kept watch over it. We stopped somewhat short of the porte-cochère where by rights there should have been a line of servants bobbing and curtseying.

Wells slipped the Jeep in between a black Mercedes sedan and a red Porsche. Across from us were a beat-up Toyota and a workman's truck.

As we walked up to the front door, I noticed the license plate on the Mercedes: MD Wells. If that was the car he'd left unattended, I could understand its being broken into. Besides being a magnet in itself, it suggested the possibility of drugs with its MD plate.

The door had been left unlocked. Opening it, Wells motioned me ahead into a wide, gloomy hall. I half expected to find a suit of armor on guard.

"Everybody's probably out back," he said. "Let me show you where you're bunking."

I followed him up a broad staircase, then along a corridor past a couple of bedrooms to the one meant for me. It apparently did double duty as a sewing room; an old-fashioned sewing machine with ornate wrought iron underpinnings stood against one wall, a chair drawn up before it. Like most of the furniture I'd glimpsed in the house so far, the bed was antique—a kind of dark Dutch or Jacobean piece, entirely lacking, for me, in period charm. I set my bag and racket case on the luggage rack at its foot. My host gave a quick look around, to see that everything was in order. Leaving, he said, "Come out whenever you're ready. You go through the kitchen."

The kitchen, airy, up to the minute, with a central island of sinks, stove and work surfaces, was larger than my living room. I paused to admire it and say hello to a fresh-faced young woman scraping carrots—a colleen not too long on these shores, to judge by the lilt of her speech—before passing through a screened porch onto a flower-bordered terrace. Here, under an awning, I found the assembled cast of characters lolling on chrome-and-plastic chairs and chaises. Beyond them, down a slight slope, was a swimming pool. More flowers edged the steppingstones leading to the blue water. Further on, through an opening in a stand of pines, lush green hills were visible.

Where, I wondered, did the money for all this come from? Hardly from what Wells earned as the head of a laboratory, even with outside consulting fees thrown in. Maybe he'd written one of those high-priced textbooks—required reading in medical school—that keep getting revised year after year so you can't get by with second-hand copies.

At sight of me he got to his feet, took me by the elbow and steered me around. His wife, too, had risen to greet me. For someone who spent most of her time in the country Jessica Wells had a mushroomy pallor. When she gardened she probably wore long sleeves and a broad-brimmed hat as protection against the sun. Her wispy once-blond hair was on the way to washed-out white. She was thin, almost scrawny,

123

in jacket, halter and shorts, all made of a material patterned with tiny flowers. I suspected they were a product of the sewing machine upstairs.

Emily Norton, who must have been around the same age as Jessica, presented a striking contrast. Her hair had completed the transition to white, a white with sheen, and was cut to disclose the handsome shape of her head. She had healthy, rosy skin. A pale-blue sun dress complemented her coloring. Dr. Norton extended a businesslike hand to me as Wells guided me to her chaise. Her husband, Sadler Norton, in a director's chair near by, appeared considerably older, his fine face crisscrossed with lines, the knees below his Bermudas knobby. But he was still handsome and his hand when I took it was firm.

Next came Anthea Burke, a jet-maned young woman whose eyes were hidden by huge round amber shades. Little else was concealed by her two-piece black bathing suit; her legs were long and tanned and she sported a firm, full pair of breasts. Stretched out on a chaise, Anthea smiled hello. Wells had introduced her as "our neighbor." I guessed she might be the one with the tennis court.

Center trustee chairman Cliff Harron, seated, offered his hand, saying, "I know this man. Hi, Bert—hear you're doing a terrific job." He was the middle-aged-executive health-club type, tight belly, sandy hair. Norma Harron, alongside him, was Goldilocks grown up: pretty, blue eyes, friendly handshake, unpretentious . . . could still have qualified for campus queen. Her one-piece bathing suit was not conspicuously revealing; and unlike Anthea she appeared to be reclining on her chaise more for relaxation than exhibition.

The others all had drinks, and Jessica asked what I'd like. There were pitchers of orange juice and iced tea on a glass-topped table, and liquor on a slatted redwood cart. I opted for the tea. Wells pulled up a spare chair and positioned me between Sadler and Anthea. I sat down feeling overdressed in polo shirt and slacks. I didn't own Bermuda or walking shorts, but figured I could soon slip up to my room again and change to my swim trunks.

Wells had been sitting next to Emily. He returned to his

place and they resumed a discussion. Biotechnological shoptalk.

Sadler (the name was one I couldn't imagine parents conferring on a helpless infant) initiated a conversation. "Understand you're with the center."

"That's right."

"I'm not clear what it is you do."

Neither am I, I wanted to say. The most important thing I'd been working on certainly hadn't been part of the job description. I told him I dealt with the media and the public, explained research developments, wrote reports, et cetera.

"Have you talked to Emily about what she's doing?"

"Just briefly, right after I came on the job. I'd like to hear more. Maybe this weekend."

"You should make a point of it, you'll find things to write about. I'm a geologist myself. Retired."

"Geology—I took a course in college." I'd never met a geologist, except the one who taught lunkheads like me.

He may have seen me trying to think what to say next on the subject—or maybe he just liked to reminisce. "Mexico . . . my first assignment. Petroleum. Petroleum my specialty. Later, Spanish government hired me to tell 'em if they had oil deposits. Spent a lot of time in Spain."

"And did they?"

"Just in trees. Olive oil."

I felt I ought to acknowledge the presence of Anthea on my other side and turned to her. "Dr. Wells said you're a neighbor. Does that mean your acres are right up against their acres?"

Why did it come out sexy? Because Anthea was sexy? Was I still capable of blushing? Was I blushing now?

"We share a stone fence." Her voice had a smoky timbre. I wished I could see her eyes behind the shades; they might give a clue to whether she thought what I'd said was sexy too. She went on: "Your work sounds interesting." She'd heard what I'd told Sadler.

"It has been so far."

"You haven't been there very long?"

"Started this summer."

"And before that?"

"Oh, freelancing. Earlier I was with a magazine called *Physicians Quarterly*. I used to be a newspaper man."

"I admire newspaper men."

"You do?"

"Who, what, where, when and why. Being able to put it all together . . ."

"It's not that hard." As I said it, it struck me that putting who, what, where, when and why together was what I'd been attempting in regard to Frawley and Dixon . . . and it was damned hard.

"Time for another swim," said Anthea suddenly, sitting up. "Care to join me?"

"Sure. I'll go change. Excuse me," I said to Sadler. I got to my feet. I watched Anthea as she removed her dark glasses and laid them on a small table next to her chaise from which she took a white rubber cap to pull on over her hair. When she started toward the pool, her buttocks rose and fell with each step contrapuntally. She hadn't been facing my way at any point and I still hadn't got a look at her eyes.

When I came down from my room I saw she was lying on her back, floating. I went straight to poolside, past the terrace group, not wanting to expose my midriff (still not tight enough, despite gym) any longer than necessary. I hoped that, once in the water, it would hardly show.

Not having been swimming for a while, and never having developed a style, I would have liked to sit for a minute on the edge, feet dangling, toes testing the water, and then ease in. But what kind of impression would that make? Overcoming my reluctance, I went to the deep end and dove.

My belly whopper attracted her attention, causing her to turn over and paddle in place. I swam to her side and trod water.

"Feels good," I said. "First time this summer."

She started moving and I stroked along beside her. At the end we turned and backed up against the tile, again treading water. "This is quite a spread," I said. "I know Ralph is good at what he does, but I had no idea . . ."

Anthea favored me with a frontal glance. "Jessica's loaded. She's a Cathcart." Cathcart Industries. Ah. Given that, fifteen acres and a pool was quite modest.

I'd gotten a look into Anthea's eyes before she thrust forward and swam off again. They were green like deep water and made me think, pleasurably, of drowning.

After I'd been in for ten or twelve minutes, she was ready to come out. I followed. I was ready for a chaise. Norma Harron had gone indoors so I took hers, offhandedly covering my middle with the bath towel I'd brought from my room. I was now next to Cliff Harron. He was determinedly cordial, and we had the center to talk about, so that kept us busy for a while.

Eventually I got up for a refill of iced tea, and this time sat down next to Jessica. She seemed basically a shy person to whom chitchat didn't come easily. After a bit I played the good guest and said I'd heard she was a wonderful gardener and maybe she'd like to show me around.

"Are you sure you . . . ?"

"Definitely—or I could go take a look myself."

"No, if you really are interested . . ." She rose, I rose, and we stepped off the terrace. Instead of heading for the pool, she turned right. Around the corner of the house there was a large flower garden, ablaze like an impressionist painting. A narrow path curved through. Leading me along it, Jessica came alive. Naming the flowers, she cooed and whispered to them, congratulating some on doing so well, urging others to try harder. Once she smiled at me with a hint of embarrassment. "Ralph tells me it's silly to talk to the flowers, but they do better this way. I can't prove it but I know it."

I was trying to think of a reply when she said, "I *can* prove it with vegetables. Over there." She nodded to a fenced-in patch a bit further to the right. When we got to the spot and started picking our way through the rows, she stopped before a lineup of cabbages, each as big as a man's head. "These I talked to," she announced. Growing in the same row but noticeably smaller were a dozen other cabbages. "These I ignored," she said. "I had to force myself because I was sure they would suffer—and they did. Even Ralph would have to admit that it was a scientific, controlled experiment."

"And did he?"

She shrugged. "He would never come look."

I was getting fond of this fey soul. When we'd finished with

the vegetables, we altered course, going down along the deep
end of the swimming pool, through some trees, to a rock
garden. A little stream ran through it, providing the justifi-
cation for a diminutive arched wooden bridge. The base of
a tall maple was circled by a rustic bench. Without striving
for total authenticity, the garden achieved a Japanese effect.

Jessica let me know, without allowing herself to brag, that
she had laid out the gardens personally and now maintained
them unaided.

"You must be out here all day every day," I said.

"Except when it's pouring rain."

We were walking slowly on the path just wide enough for
two. Suddenly Jessica stopped and said, "You're trying to
find Faith?"

It was a little surprising to realize this person had some
idea what was going on outside her constricted private world.

"To find her—or find out what happened to her."

"Ralph's very upset."

"I know." A faint hope arose in me that Jessica might have
some light to throw on the mystery.

"We used to see her up here, and then it stopped," she said.

"Why is that?"

"Well, Emily Norton was her thesis adviser . . . that was
quite a while ago . . . and sometimes they'd be here on the
same weekend. That was all right at first, until Emily got the
idea that Faith was in love with her husband. . . ."

Sadler. If he was handsome now in old age, he must have
been beautiful then.

"Was she, do you think?" Maybe I was getting a line to
something significant.

"Perhaps. She certainly seemed to idolize him, she hung
on his every word."

"So on account of Emily you stopped inviting her, is that
it?"

"I would have been willing to go on having her here. She
could have come when the Nortons didn't. But Ralph said it
would be a mistake."

I tried to imagine what bearing this ancient history could
have had on current events, but nothing suggested itself. And

128

I could hardly ask Jessica if she thought the Nortons had had anything to do with Faith's dropping out of sight.

She started to walk again. We followed a circuitous route back to the house, approaching by way of the swimming pool. Pausing there, I remarked on the wonderful view of the hills through the pine trees—the same view you saw from the terrace. Bitterly, Jessica said, "Yes, the view is so important Ralph can't stop cutting down trees. He always finds more that are in the way." She added vehemently, "Trees have rights!"

That was the Jessica I'd so quickly grown fond of . . . and now, sorry for.

By the time we'd completed our tour a good forty minutes had elapsed and Ralph was no longer outdoors with the others.

"He's in the study," Norma said in response to Jessica's questioning look. "Some work he's got to do."

I hoped it was the work I'd come here about.

He reappeared at cocktail time, after the rest of us—not counting Anthea, who'd left for the day—had changed for dinner and were reassembled on the terrace. Stopping briefly at my side, he said in a low voice, "You may be right. I've been looking at the books . . . I'm not sure of the full extent yet."

Well, at least he'd started. But how long would it take him to read enough to be able to reach a conclusion?

Cliff Harron, according to Sadler Norton, made the perfect martini, and we all had one, except for Jessica. It *was* damn good. So was the wine when we filed into the dining room an hour later. Again, Jessica did not drink.

The table at which we had our dinner was beautifully laid with the finest china and silver. Spaced equidistant from either end were two matching silver candlesticks topped with branched candelabra each bearing a pair of lighted candles. Ornate but elegant and clearly of great value. Very likely the candlesticks stolen out of Wells's car trunk, recovered and, presumably, restored to pristine perfection by the master in Brighton Beach.

After dinner, as we drifted into the living room where a

card table was set up, Jessica said, "I know you'll excuse me, I have to go out."

Sadler, in what he doubtless thought was a whisper but which must have carried past the ear for which it was intended (mine), explained, "She's in AA."

No one gave any indication of having heard—and I imagined it was old news to them anyway.

I wondered what had driven her to drink—whether it might have been Ralph.

The card table was there for poker. I had thought I'd spend some time talking to Emily Norton—not only for news of her research that I ought to be broadcasting, but for whatever I might learn that pertained to Faith. When it turned out she was going to play, I got in on the game too. The Harrons and our host completed the party.

I'm a pretty good poker player but Emily was sharper. By the time Jessica got home again and the game broke up, she'd won forty-eight dollars and I was out ten.

I now sat down with Emily for a discussion of what she was working on.

"AIDS is the toughest problem I ever tackled," she said. "I'm afraid I may not live to see a solution." There was a lot of interesting stuff going on in her lab, but nothing she considered worth reporting.

About the building-fund campaign she felt more sanguine. Her fellow scientists had closed ranks around her after Dixon's death and several had upped their pledges.

I asked if she thought Dixon was murdered, and whether it might have been by someone opposed to the expansion program.

"I have no idea," she said. "I doubt he fell off that balcony. I'm never confident I know anybody well enough to rule out suicide."

Then, while I was speculating on how she felt about taking Dixon's place, she added, "If there's some sociopath out there waiting to knock me off next, I won't go gently, I can tell you that much."

Disingenuously I asked, "Did you know Faith Frawley?"

"Yes. You're supposed to be working on that, aren't you? Have they found out anything yet?"

"Not that I know of."

"The poor woman . . . there was something not quite right about her. Very bright in her work . . . gifted . . . but she had trouble with relationships."

"In the laboratory?"

"I can't speak to that. But outside. I was her thesis adviser— that was quite a while ago. She used to complain about her parents—father especially. He had no comprehension of what she was about . . . why she wanted to leave home and study science. I think she spent her life looking for a sympathetic father."

It fitted in with what Jessica had told me, adding a little more depth. Emily undoubtedly had been jealous of Faith, perhaps with reason. But could something have happened to reactivate that jealousy at this late date? And if so, was Emily a suspect in Faith's disappearance?

Sunday morning the Harrons, Nortons and I were lounging around on the terrace sharing two copies of the *Times* provided by the thoughtful management. Norma and I were doing our separate crossword puzzles, breaking our silence every so often to ask the other for help. Jessica was believed to be gardening; there had been no formal breakfast, each person selecting from a buffet when he or she was ready to eat, and Jessica presumably had risen before any of us. Ralph had just been getting up from the dining table when I came downstairs. "Got to get back to those books," he said and was gone.

The day was bright and hot again and getting hotter when Ralph returned. I'd finished as much of the puzzle as I could and was reading the letters to the editor, usually the best part of the paper. He came over to me. "Bert, how about a little walk?"

I was on my feet fast. We took the route down to the pool.

"I read some more this morning," he began. "There are some discrepancies . . . a few gaps. Regrettable. Our laboratory has always prided itself on its accuracy. I don't, however, think there was any intention here to deceive. Let's say carelessness . . . being in a hurry. Whether it was Faith in the first place, and Gordon tagging along, or the other way around—

or both of them anxious to make a name for themselves—I
don't believe they were trying to pull the wool over anybody's
eyes. I'll expect an explanation from Gordon, of course, but
I can imagine what it'll be: they were so sure they were on
the right track that they wanted to get the word out before
anyone else beat them to it. They'd fill in the gaps later."

"But that's not—" I started to say.

"I know, it's not acceptable procedure, so maybe the police
theory is correct: maybe Faith did suffer an attack of conscience—maybe a breakdown of some sort—and went away
for a while. I hope it's only for a while. Because as I went over
the workbooks and the *Cell* paper (I've just read it again), no
harm's been done—it can all be set straight. Even so, I'm
going to have Gordon write to the journal and apologize for
jumping the gun. And I'm going to take my share of the
blame: I shouldn't have put my name to the damn thing, or
let it go through, without doing what I've just done—give it
my full attention. And I have you to thank for that . . . and
do thank you."

Clever fox, Ralph. I suspected he'd found more twisting of
the truth in those "discrepancies" than he was letting on and
that now his main concern was damage control. That meant
I was to be patted on the head and diverted from the pursuit.

I could understand his taking this tack. If there was a possible scandal in the making, nip it. If the *Cell* report was as
phony as I imagined, full disclosure of its dishonesty could
deal Ralph's reputation a serious blow.

By admitting as much as he had about Gordon's (and
Faith's?) transgression, he had bolstered my theory that Barnard had got rid of Faith—and quite likely Dixon. This
would eliminate Emily Norton as a suspect. But I was still
far from proving anything.

Furthermore, I was sure Ralph would take the first opportunity to warn Barnard that his fraudulent science had been
discovered. If Barnard was, additionally, responsible for
Faith's disappearance, he'd have advance notice that he might
fall under suspicion for that crime—which could make it
more difficult, if not impossible, to trap him.

I'd have to think of some move to take without fucking
everything up. Fast.

Ralph was interpreting my lack of objection to his proposed procedure as acceptance. He would mildly chastise
Barnard, get them both off the hook with *Cell*'s readers and
let it go at that. Changing the subject with what must have
been intense relief, he said, "Anthea's expecting us over at
her place for tennis and a light lunch."

"Fine. When does she want us?"

He glanced at his watch. "Ten after eleven now. We can go
as soon as everyone's ready."

We turned back toward the house, ostensibly in agreement
about what was to be done regarding Gordon Barnard.

Half an hour later the Harrons, Nortons, Ralph and I
arrived in two cars at Anthea's. I'd ridden with Ralph, just
the two of us. On the way he'd turned almost fatherly, voicing
concern over how much time and effort I'd invested in trying
to solve the Faith puzzle. "I think you're letting it take over,"
he said. "You should be building a life for yourself—make
new friends in New York. Do you have a steady lady friend?"

"I don't know how steady."

"You should be playing the field."

This was getting too intimate; I didn't like it. "Am I going
to meet Anthea's husband?"

"No, he's away." Thank God we'd gotten off my love life.

A Henry Moore and a Calder were among the sculptures
gracing Anthea's driveway. The house, a low-lying contemporary, all cedar and glass, provided a stylish background for
its chatelaine who was awaiting us out front. Again the amber
shades plus a white cloth hat topping the cascading black
hair. This time those shapely long legs extended from a mini-
mal white pleated skirt.

"Would you like to play a set before we eat?" she asked.

We all trooped around to the back where there was a covered patio and a fine clay court. It seemed logical for the
two husband-and-wife couples to start off, so Anthea, Ralph
and myself took our places on the sidelines in comfortable
mesh chairs, Anthea in the middle.

I asked, "Who's the art collector? You or your husband,
or both?"

"I am. Hank's learned to like most of it, but basically he's
indulging me."

"What's Hank do?"

"Civil engineer. He's in Lima at the moment."

"I think there are certain places he ought to steer clear of," said Ralph, "and that's one of them."

"I've stopped worrying," Anthea said. She turned to me. "Did you do the puzzle? I know Ralph never does."

"The crossword? Yes, most of it."

"Did you get twelve across?"

"Ozymandias?"

"I'll go see." She got up, went indoors and returned a minute later with the *Times* magazine and a pencil. Sitting down, she counted letters and spaces. "You're a genius"—and started filling them in.

Ralph asked, "Is the gym unlocked? I think Bert ought to see it."

"If it isn't, the key's under the bottom step on the right."

"Hank's built himself the perfect place to work out. How long does he spend every day, Anthy?"

"Two hours."

"He must be in great shape," I said.

Ralph had got to his feet. I did likewise.

"He's not here every day, though, even when he's home. We have an apartment in the city."

The gym was a separate one-story structure behind the capacious garage. The door proved to be unlocked. Ralph motioned me in ahead of him. It was, as he'd said, a perfect place to work out ... not unlike Midtown Boxing on a smaller scale. The space looked to be about twenty-five by thirty feet. Equipment included a stairclimber, treadmill, weight machine, bars, stationary bike, punching bag and basketball hoop with ball ready to hand on the floor below. Every home should have such a gym.

I did a trial run on the stairclimber while Ralph picked up the ball, dribbled and tried for a basket—succeeding on the third attempt.

"Hey, let's put these on." He'd spotted two pairs of gloves on a ledge. "I understand you're a fighter."

"Where'd you hear that?"

Dropping the ball back where he'd found it: "You knocked

some guy out at that big protest meeting—everybody was talking about it."

"Guy was drunk. I knocked him—but not out."

"I used to do a little boxing in school. Here—" He tossed me one pair. They were without laces, elasticized on the bottom so a solo puncher could put them on unaided. "We don't have to get serious," Ralph went on, "but we can trade a few."

"Okay." I didn't feel much like absorbing any punishment and I certainly didn't want to inflict any.

I was wearing slacks, he was in shorts. We removed our shirts and got into the gloves. Moving to the center of the room, we started circling each other, dancing. While this was going on, Anthea glided quietly in. The sight of her put me off for a second, just long enough for Ralph to deliver a poke to the plexus. It squeezed a bit of air out of me, but also triggered a reaction—a right to his jaw. A little harder than I'd intended, but he took it gamely.

After that we both feinted, dancing again, I feeling faintly ridiculous in front of Anthea. Then he landed one on my upper left arm. I got a couple of jabs in, one just below the collar bone, followed by another to the jaw.

For a minute after that we traded a quick series of punches. It seemed to me if we didn't watch it we could start fighting in earnest. Between irritation and exasperation, I delivered a solid punch to his belly. Again, I hadn't meant to hit so hard—or maybe I did.

He threw up his hands. "Help!" Gasping.

Lowering mine, I said, "Did I hurt you?"

"No, no—it's all right. But you've got power there, boy."

"I didn't mean—"

"Don't apologize—you're a lot better than I am!"

"It's Bloody Mary time," said Anthea. "Come cool off."

"Be right there," said Ralph.

Soon we were seated under the awning with the rest of the party, whetting our appetites with the spicy drinks. As we worked our way toward refills, the women set out lunch on a table, and soon we were loading our plates with Niçoise from a huge glass salad bowl and with our choice of cheeses, breads and assorted other goodies. Then back to our comfortable chairs. High life.

135

Paul Nathan

After lunch I figured it was my turn for tennis, but Ralph had a different idea. "Anthy, why don't you show Bert what Hank collects? It's fabulous," he said to me.

"Yes, come take a look." She rose. I followed her into the house.

The inside was what you'd expect from the outside: sleek furniture and pictures, mostly abstract, that looked like big-name stuff to me. I wasn't sure I'd like to live in it; it was handsome but very cool.

She led me through the living room into a long hall, all the way to the end. En route I glanced through open doors and saw that one room had posters of baseball and football stars on the walls. Also sophisticated construction toys on a shelf.

"You have a son?" We had stopped at the last door.

"Daughter. Away in camp."

I stepped into the room after her. At first glance it seemed like too many television sets to have in one place. Then I realized they were not current models, and as I turned to take in the whole array the strangeness of some of them struck me. "Your husband collects TV sets? Are they all old?" A few of them had a futuristic look.

"Yes, and the funny thing is, the ones that look like Tomorrow World are actually the oldest." She moved to a tall cabinet with a big eye at the top. "This is so tall because the earliest tubes had such long necks. Here"—stepping over to another model—"is a thirty-five-inch tube . . . still the largest black-and-white ever made. Dumont, 1950."

We went from one to another; there must have been twenty-two or -three. Several dated from the Thirties—even the late Twenties.

While I was admiring a Baird (1936, England—Anthea really knew the stock), I felt a gentle pressure against my lower back. Then what could only be a pelvic grind. I turned, and met her hands on my belly.

Automatically, my hands went around *her* back, just above her cheeks. We pressed together.

"You're a very attractive man," she whispered. Must be my boxing.

"You're gorgeous," I replied, sincerely.

136

Oddly, in spite of the sexy. voluptuous way she'd been flaunting her enticements, her pass had come as a surprise. For a moment I was taken aback, then I thought What the hell—*wow!*, let's get on with it.

Taking my hand, she led me to the door and across the hall where another door stood closed. As she turned the knob she said conspiratorially, "Maid's room. We're between maids." And, leading the way in, "If anyone comes looking they'll never think of in here."

Inside, the blind was drawn, the light was dim gray.

"Shut the door," she said.

I did. The bed, neatly made up, was narrow. No point spoiling the maid, when there was one. But narrow would be wide enough for our purposes.

Then I thought of something. The thing you always had to think about nowadays in casual sex—especially with someone like this hot number.

"You don't really know me," I said, tactfully. "Do you have a condom?"

She reached into the slit pocket of her little skirt and produced one in its packet.

At that moment suspicion struck. Wells had paired me off with her, knowing her proclivities. The fact that she was prepared with a condom suggested that she'd been tipped off to what he had in mind. It was a put-up job. Anthea was a bribe—an inducement, if one was needed, for me to go easy about the fraud.

Whether Anthea herself had any notion that she was part of a quid pro quo I couldn't tell, but all at once my arousal gave way to anger. I felt myself shrivel and knew I wouldn't be able to perform.

Should I make an attempt anyway?

She was slipping the halter from her shoulders, fully exposing her ripe, luscious twosome.

"Look," I said. "I'm sorry. This isn't going to work."

She stood staring.

"I want you," I stumbled on, "but I can't. Not now."

I turned and fled—back to the tennis court where the rest of the party were sitting around.

Wells walked over to me, searched my face, trying to gauge what had gone on in the house. I suppressed all expression.

"How's that for a collection?" he said, still trying.

"Fabulous."

"And she's the one knows how to show it, eh?" He took my arm and gave it a suggestive pinch.

Anthea had come out. "Now it's time for the two of you to play," Wells said. "Where's your racket?"

"Over there. But I think—not right now."

She was listening. "Not now?" She picked her racket up from a chaise."You can't *play tennis* now?"

There was no way to avoid this one. A minute later the two of us were facing across the net.

We played. She beat the shit out of me.

SIXTEEN

The afternoon following my country weekend Hazel joined me in the cafeteria. Eve was away at her conference. The last time I'd discussed The Case with Hazel I'd been exploring the possibility that different labs might be competing for funds and space in the new construction, and that Frawley and Dixon could have been victims of the rivalry. The idea that Barnard might have been Frawley's lover and killer hadn't yet hit me.

Today when I introduced this new theory Hazel was rocked. "Jesus," was all she could say at first. Her eyes moved away from me to people at the other tables. When she spoke again it was as though she was seeing things in a new light. "Unreal. You look around you, everything's so normal. If Gordon Barnard were sitting at the next table he'd look as normal as anybody."

"Maybe he is."

"That's what's so scary."

"By now Wells will have told him that the police think Faith might have gone AWOL over the phony research results. That means Gordon knows he's under a cloud as her collaborator. And if he was her murderer, he's going to have his guard up every minute. He and Constance are getting married any day now. It's bad enough she should marry a liar, but a murderer . . . ? How do we stall the wedding and get at the truth?"

She considered the question carefully. "You've got to take him by surprise."

"Okay, but how?"

Another pause while she sat thinking. Thinking hard, her hand held, fisted, to her chin. Finally she said, "When I was on the *Record* . . . there were times I had to get a story and the one person who could confirm something wouldn't talk." I nodded in recognition.

"If you were fairly sure of your ground," she went on, "you acted like you already had the evidence and *you* told *them* the facts. At least that's how *I* played it—hoping I was right. Then they thought there was no point in holding out any longer and they caved in. Sometimes. If you were lucky."

"Yes, that's it. That's what I've got to do here."

"It's a gamble—but if you don't have any alternative . . . Look, I think I know how to work it. How do you stand with the cops on the Frawley case?"

"There're two detectives I've been dealing with—Holsclaw and Sanchez. They might go along with something that looked like it'd pay off."

"See what you think of this." And she proceeded to outline a plan of action.

It would mean using Wells to make it happen but deceiving him—not letting him know what was really going on. He'd catch on soon enough, and when he did he'd hate it—and hate me. Unless it got results. Which it had to or I'd be out on the street. Then he'd be grateful to me, the way he'd pretended to be about my tipping him off to the fraud. Only this time it would be genuine.

"I'll do it—if I can convince the cops . . . and if I can con Wells into cooperating."

"When do you think . . . ?"

"I'll try for tomorrow."

It took me most of the afternoon to reach Sanchez on the phone. His partner was out.

"I want to know if you and Holsclaw are game to put on a little show for Gordon Barnard's benefit."

"You mean like to catch the conscience of the king?"

Not for the first time I wondered at the surprises of New York. He got the drift of my startled silence. "I acted in college."

"Yes, that *is* what I mean. In a general way."

"I can't speak for Holsclaw, but if it sounds reasonable . . ."

"Here's the scheme: We meet in Dr. Wells' office—Bar-

nard works for Wells. I got Wells to check out Barnard's research—the experiments he did with Faith Frawley. It turned
out just like I thought—some of the stuff was faked. I don't
know how much—I get the impression it's more than Wells
admits. He doesn't know I think Barnard killed Frawley—
probably over this fakery and the affair he was breaking off.
But I've told him that you guys have a theory—"

"Me and Holsclaw?"

"Yeah, I was sure you wouldn't mind, and now it turns out
you're an actor . . . you'll enjoy playing your part."

"So what's this theory supposed to be?"

"Frawley got guilt pangs—she'd let her ambition run away
with her up to the point where the phony stuff was going to
be published, then she panicked. Most research cheating's
never discovered; there're too many scientific journals, too
many experiments for other people to try to duplicate, so
most of the cheaters get away with it. But Frawley's basically
straight. She went overboard for a while—maybe because
Barnard led her into it. Then she couldn't face the possibility
of exposure and took a powder."

"We thought all this up?"

"I explained to Wells that you guys are sharp and with all
this scientific fraud in the news lately, you came up with a
scenario that—"

"Okay, let's say we're with you so far. What's our act?"

"I go to Wells and tell him you'd like to get together with
Barnard. I'll be there, Wells'll be there and Fumi Tashamira—she was Frawley's friend at the lab. Wells thinks you
just want to talk to Barnard about the research—and that
once you hear him admit it was doctored, you'll be satisfied
that your theory about Frawley's vanishing act was probably
right. Then you'll stop trying to figure out what happened
to her. I think Wells has accepted that she's gone for good
and he's tired of all this poking around for clues.

"Actually, what's going to happen is that when we have
Barnard sitting in the hot seat, you and Dr. Tashamira and
I are going to pull a big bluff. It's the way I used to get
people to admit things when I was a reporter and I knew
they were hiding something and I was pretty sure what." I
didn't think Hazel would mind me appropriating her idea;

after all, I'd used it myself on the job. "I'd come at them like I already had the dope from somewhere else and I'd tell them what it was, and if it was true they'd think the jig was up."

"What if it wasn't true?"

"In this case I'm certain it is."

"And if it is and still doesn't work?"

"The investigation's getting no place anyway and the big loser will be me."

"Like having to look for other employment?"

"You got it."

"You're willing to stake everything . . ."

"I want to bring that sonofabitch Barnard down."

"Have you talked to this Dr. Takish . . . ?"

"Tashamira. Not yet. I wanted to get you lined up first."

"Well, I'll have to sell it to Holsclaw. Incidentally, who writes our dialogue?"

"You do—the two of you. At the proper time—and you'll know when that is—you'll come up with a story about finding one of Frawley's missing suitcases, or both of them—"

"In the East River?"

"Right. With her inside . . . what's left of her. I'll leave it to you to put it in your own words. Tashamira'll already have lied that Frawley'd told her Barnard was coming to see her that Saturday night—to settle something between them. Wells has socked it to him about the phony research. Then you say they dragged up a suitcase, and we've got the guy on the ropes." I had a further thought: "Shall I get over to the precinct and brief Holsclaw myself?"

"I don't think so. He's not big on playacting. He likes to have all his ducks in a row—the real evidence before he moves. And he's not the most flexible guy in the world. So it's going to take someone who's worked with him and knows him to bring him around. Better let me handle it."

"And you think you *can* bring him around?"

"Do my damnedest."

I contacted Fumi on the phone in the lab and asked her to come see me in my office. Without clueing her in to my suspicion of Barnard as murderer, I told her she could help solve the mystery of Faith if she'd stretch the truth a little. Faith had confided in her that she was having a showdown with someone. I was about ninety-nine percent certain it was Barnard. What I wanted was for Fumi to say to Barnard's face that Faith had identified him as the person she was expecting. Would she do that?

"You say it's in a good cause," she said. "Yes."

Next I got Wells to agree to a meeting the next afternoon in his office, leaving it up to him to see that Barnard would attend. I didn't mention that Fumi would be there because I didn't want to have to explain her presence in advance.

That night Eve called me from Atlanta. How had my weekend gone? had I pinned anything on Gordon? "Fraud," I said. "—And maybe worse to come. I'll tell you all about it when you get back—there ought to be more to tell by then. How's the conference?"

"It's the first one in years where we really have something to talk about—now that the government's stirred things up."

"And how was Robert's girlfriend?"

"Just as nice as she sounded on the phone."

"Glad to hear it. Have a good time in Fort Worth."

Six was a crowd in Wells's office. Before he'd had a chance to open his mouth about Fumi I said, "I asked Dr. Tashamira to join us." And that was that.

Everyone seemed to have dressed with special care, as though for a day in court. Barnard had on a lightweight gray suit; Wells had donned his jacket for a change and even wore a tie. The two detectives—Sanchez darkly good-looking, Holsclaw red-faced and straining against his belt—appeared less wilted than when they'd called on me, no doubt because this wasn't as hot or as humid a day. Fumi was in a freshly starched lab coat. I was wearing my pin stripe navy-blue summer suit, the one for serious occasions; I hoped I looked prosecutorial.

When we were all settled down, Wells began, "It was Bert's idea that we get together, and I'm going to let him start."

I sat up straight and addressed Barnard. "I'm sure you know, Gordon, that there's a question about your research—yours and Faith's."

"Yes, we went ahead and announced something before it was fully documented. But in our defense I'd like to point out that what we did was hardly unusual."

"We realize that," I replied. "There's been a lot of it lately."

"Not only lately! This is one area where I've really done my research. Let me tell you! Ptolemy—supposed to be one of the great pioneers in astronomy. He stole data that he passed off as his own and faked a lot of the rest! Darwin we now know plagiarized from someone named Edward Blyth. Mendel altered the statistics on garden peas to prove what he was sure was correct. And Newton—! Revised later editions of his *Principia* to make the measurements look more accurate than they really were. Not only that: when he was president of the Royal Society he pushed through a report claiming he'd invented calculus. Leibnitz said *he* had. The report was supposed to have been written by a committee, but it turned out Newton wrote it himself. Then there's Galileo. Somebody asked if he'd really dropped a ball from the mast of a moving ship to see how it fell, and he said he didn't have to—he already knew the answer!"

Boy, I thought, you certainly did do your research—all of it, probably, since Wells warned you yesterday you were going to be called on the carpet. I couldn't help admiring the slick sonofabitch.

Sanchez and Holsclaw were exchanging glances, not knowing what to make of this virtuoso performance.

"You realize we're not planning to throw you in jail for tricking up your report," I said.

"No? Then what's this all about? I admitted to Dr. Wells that we'd jumped the gun and I've told him I'd put it in writing for *Cell*. Maybe someone'll tell me what these detectives are doing here."

"I will," I said. I was sure Wells had already done so, but what the hell. "They're on Dr. Frawley's case and think they have the answer to what happened and that you may be able to confirm it. They've got her down as a person of strict standards who maybe got carried away and put her name to a report that was, shall we say, a bit premature. They think she panicked when she realized it was really going to be published and certain things about it might have to be documented, and she ran. If that's true and she disappeared of her own volition, the police can drop the investigation."

I was watching Barnard closely and there was a perceptible relaxation in his face and body as he took in this last statement.

I added, "They have reason to believe you were in a position to know if Faith might have taken a powder."

"Why me?"

"Dr. Tashamira . . ." I nodded to Fumi.

She turned to Barnard. "That Friday, the weekend she disappeared, she said you were coming to see her the next night. And she spoke of a showdown of some sort. I couldn't imagine what about . . . I always saw you working together, it looked like you got along. Well, she didn't say what about and I didn't ask. It was none of my business."

My eyes were still on Barnard; he was tense again, a cord in his neck had tightened. I felt he felt cornered, having to make a fast judgment: would it prove safer for him to admit he'd been with Faith Saturday night or to deny it?

Finally he said, "Yes, we saw each other, because we wanted to talk, but I wouldn't have thought of it as a showdown."

At which point Holsclaw put in his first words: "Well, what did you want to talk about?"

"The extrapolation of research results. Bert's right, she wasn't too happy about that."

"The ex— The what?" said Sanchez. I had no doubt he knew the word, but he gave the impression he was aiming for, of being not quite on top of things.

"Extrapolation. We were sure the way Galileo was sure— we knew where we were going, so we put down a few figures that clinched it. We were planning to do the backup very soon. If Faith hadn't— Well, it would all be done by now. I told her it was silly of her to get so excited. After all, Dr. Wells's name was on the paper as principal investigator. If there was any trouble, which was unlikely, he'd be in it with us, and people would go easy. . . ."

Very smart of Barnard, covering himself this way; but Wells didn't like it. "Of course I'd take my share of responsibility," he said, in a tone to discourage involving him further in a sticky situation. "But I must point out my responsibility

145

is limited to not having reviewed the research as thoroughly as I should have."

Barnard, too, as I read it, was now getting a feeling of being trapped and he didn't want to be left holding the bag alone. "According to Faith," he shot at Wells, "you knew and approved of what we were doing!"

"That's not true!" Wells flushed. With an effort he took control of himself; when he next spoke, it was calmly. "Either you misunderstood or she was leading you on for reasons of her own."

Barnard was not buying this. He glared.

"Look," said Wells, "we're letting ourselves get riled up." Minor disagreement at best, his tone indicated. He referred to his watch. "Almost five o'clock—I suggest we take a little refreshment break."

He opened his bottom desk drawer. "Fumi, those glasses right behind you . . . want to pass them over?" While she was reaching for them, he drew up a bottle and set it down in front of him.

Tullamore Dew.

Seeing the label was like being kicked in the gut.

"There's supposed to be ice in that silver bucket," Wells said.

Sanchez picked the bucket up and handed it to Holsclaw, who set it down on the desk. Wells poured the first drink. "Fumi?"

"Oh, that's too much. Please, just half."

He held it out toward Holsclaw, who said, "Sorry, no thanks. On duty."

As Sanchez waved it away, Wells offered it to Barnard, who ignored it. I accepted it, hoping my shaking hand wouldn't be noticed. Barnard was saying to the detectives, "If you want to know do I think Dr. Frawley was sufficiently upset to pack up and go off some place, I guess the answer is yes. I didn't realize it at the time. After I told her it was too late to stop publication, and we'd make our claims good later, she quieted down. I thought she'd decided to accept what she couldn't change."

He swung around, facing Wells. "And I want to correct an impression if anybody here has it. I was the junior member of the team; Faith was the one who set the course, I followed along." He turned back to Sanchez and Holsclaw again. "She was hellbent to have something to show for her years in the lab—she'd worked a long time and felt she wasn't getting anywhere. Then, when she was about to be in the spotlight, she froze up. She saw the down side of going public with something that wasn't all there. So yes, she probably got stage-fright and found herself a place to hide. Maybe she'll come out some day. I hope so. Now, is there anything else I can do for you gentlemen?"

This would be the cue for them to spring their lie about the suitcases and body parts—but now I was no longer sure where guilt lay. Was it Barnard that Faith kept the Tullamore Dew for, or could it have been Wells? Or both? I needed time to think before letting the boys play their trump card. Once played, it could never be used again.

I stood and moved between Barnard and the detectives. "Dr. Barnard has told us what we came to hear," I said. "Now I think we can call it a day."

My co-conspirators reacted with perfect aplomb. They thanked Barnard, they thanked Wells, they thanked us all for our cooperation. As soon as they had left, Barnard stalked out, obviously still angry.

I overtook him in the adjoining lab just as he was leaving. I could see he was holding in his rage; I felt there'd never be a better time for me to take advantage of what he was feeling.

"You needed a drink in there," I said. "So did I. But I was too upset to finish mine—it looked like if things got rough, Wells was ready to make you the fall guy."

"You saw that?"

"Couldn't miss it. And things *could* get rough, still."

I'd caught his attention. "You think so?"

"I wouldn't trust those cops. I'm not at all sure they believe their own theory about Faith. More likely trying to get something on you. Let's have that drink—I'll buy us a taxi, there's a place near World Wide Plaza. Nobody we know ever goes there."

I had him on a lead and he came docilely along.

SEVENTEEN

It was a Japanese restaurant where you could drink either at the bar or one of the nearby tables spaced far enough apart to insure privacy. Shoji screens, dim lighting. And at this hour, only the bartender and a single bar patron, male, conversing in Japanese.

The bartender came around, over to our table. "Gordon, what are you having?" I asked. He didn't bother to inquire about his pet brand, figuring they wouldn't stock it and it would be wasting precious time; he really needed his drink. "Irish on the rocks?" he said, with a rising inflection. Maybe they wouldn't even have Irish? But the bartender took it in stride, nodded and looked at me.

"Make that two." When we were alone again I waited to see what question would come up first.

It was "Why would they be wanting to get something on me? That's what you said."

I shrugged. "I don't know. Maybe they don't have any other leads and you're the person who worked closest with her and they know you disagreed about something."

"A lot of people disagree about a lot of things—and our disagreement wasn't that serious. By 'get something on me,' what do you mean exactly?"

"I think maybe what *they* mean"—I took my time, letting each word sink in—"is murder."

"Murder!" He was keeping his voice to little more than a whisper, but it shook. "That's— That's ridiculous! Why would I—what reason would I have? None. None whatever."

"They're probably just fishing," I said reassuringly. Then: "You were at her place the weekend she disappeared—the last person they know of who saw her."

He looked outraged. "Is this what I do to myself by admitting I was there? By being honest? I was a fool. I should have said I didn't know what Fumi was talking about. What she thinks she heard Faith say isn't proof of anything. And why she's turned on me I don't understand! I was just trying to be cooperative, I wanted to help the investigation, and now I end up being the fall guy."

I sat silent.

"You said that's what Wells would make me."

"That's the impression I got back there a little while ago."

"You mean he'd let me take a *murder* rap? He'd go that far?"

"Gordon, I don't know if he's even thinking of murder—it may just be wanting to keep his skirts clean about the research. But I do get the feeling that as far as it took him he'd sacrifice you to protect himself."

Divide and conquer. That was a strategy as good as the one Hazel had recommended, and maybe this would carry me the rest of the way.

I also decided to spread my net wider—no telling what might get entangled in it. "I hate to say it, but there's another murder they might try to hang on you. If it was a murder. The police seem to think they're linked."

"You're not talking about Morgan Dixon?"

"Yes."

"Why? For God's sake, why? Just because nobody knows what happened and it's another mystery involving Krinsky?"

I saw no reason to provide him with a preview of the ammunition that might be used against him: the competition between his lab and Dixon's for funding and space. "It does seem pretty farfetched," I said.

"God, I wish I'd never heard of Krinsky! This is a hell of a thing to happen when I'm getting married in a couple of weeks! Suspicion of murder—two murders at that! It could ruin everything." For a minute he looked ready to cry; then he took a deep breath.

"Let me tell you something." Desperation was driving him on. "I wasn't the last person at Faith's that night. She was alive when I left."

"How do you know there was someone else after you?"

Our whiskeys were coming and nothing further was said till they were served.

He resumed eagerly. "How do I know there was someone? Faith asked me to leave. It wasn't unfriendly," he added quickly. "We were on good terms after . . . after agreeing there was nothing to be done about canceling *Cell*. I thought I'd hang around for a few minutes and have a drink but she said she was sorry, she was expecting someone else and couldn't let me stay. I said okay, no problem." He took a swallow. "But I was curious. Something about the way she was acting . . . she seemed nervous. And I don't know, maybe subconsciously I had a feeling that we'd reached an agreement but I wasn't sure she really meant it. Did she have some kind of a scheme—I don't know what it would be, but like you said about Ralph . . . some way to keep *her* skirts clean—and screw *me*?

"Anyway, after we said good night, I went downstairs and across the street, and there was an archway, a place I could stand and not be seen. I watched the door to her house, and a few people went by, and after a while along came— Get this: Ralph Wells!"

He watched for my reaction. I didn't attempt to conceal my surprise—in fact, I may have beefed it up a bit to convince him I believed what he was saying. Because I wasn't all sure that I did. It could be that if Wells was willing to make him the fall guy, he was slipping the knife in first.

But the Tullamore Dew . . . Probably one of these two had introduced it to the other, and it could have been Wells she kept that bottle for as easily as Barnard.

"He went inside?" I asked, and in reply to Barnard's nod: "Why haven't you mentioned this till now?"

"Till now I haven't heard anything about murder charges—I wasn't going to cause trouble for my boss by giving an answer to a question nobody'd asked. Why stick my neck out? We all know what happens to whistle blowers. And I was on enough of a spot—potentially anyway—with the *Cell* thing. Ralph was mixed up in that too. All three of us. Let's just say I didn't want to trouble trouble."

"I can't blame you for that," I said. "But it's a shock—the idea that Wells was there that night . . ."

"I'm not saying he did anything." Having planted his seed of doubt, Barnard was now attempting to disclaim any harmful intent.

"No, of course not. But have you any clue as to why Wells would be paying her a visit?"

"You've met Mrs. Wells?" he asked unexpectedly. The question was rhetorical; he knew where I'd spent the weekend.

"Yes."

"I was asked out to their place several times when I was new in the lab. Jessica took a shine to me—or if that wasn't it, at least I was somebody new to talk to. She said things to me like 'People think of me as this lady living a wonderful life in the country, busy with my garden and my dogs.' They had golden retrievers then. 'Ralph keeps me prisoner out here,' she said. 'What else am I supposed to do but garden and sew?' She drank a lot and when she'd had too much she'd accuse Ralph of playing around in town. I think now he had a thing going with Faith. Maybe long term, because as far as I knew she never dated."

"They *had* dogs? Then what happened?"

"Oh, one of them was crushed by a falling tree. The trees used to be so thick—there was practically a forest—and Ralph was always going out with his saw." He mimicked Wells's voice: 'I have to have vistas!' Jessica loved those dogs so; she gave the other two away. Later, someone brought her a puppy and she refused to take it."

"Power saw of course," I said.

"Yeah. Gasoline. Look, Bert, what do you think's going to happen next? With me?"

I suppressed my shiver at the possibility of a connection between Ralph's saw and Faith's disappearance. "I can't tell. Maybe nothing will happen. Looks like they don't have any evidence against you. They can't have, if you haven't done anything."

"You know those detectives. Maybe you can find out what they've got in mind?"

"I just barely know them. But sure, if they'll talk to me."

He stood abruptly and reached for his wallet. "I've got to go."

"Keep your money, I'll take care of it. I'll stay and finish my drink."

"Thanks. I don't know how much of all this to tell Connie. I don't want to upset her."

"I wouldn't tell her anything. Especially not about Ralph. If she breathes a word to her father . . . Don't complicate things, Gordon." I was trying to sound avuncular; I wanted him to think I was sympathetic.

I couldn't wait to be alone to sort out my thoughts. The saw! The instrument that had dismembered Faith . . . could it be?

Was it Wells who had been Faith's lover? If she'd always been in search of a father, Wells could have succeeded Sadler Norton. Maybe it had been Wells the whole time, with Norton covering for him, letting it appear he was the object of Faith's love.

Faith would have known Ralph's marriage was a washout. And if she thought enough of him to have stuck with him through a long liaison, why wouldn't she eventually want him to terminate that marriage and begin a new one with her? After feeding off the scraps of his life for years, it would be natural at some point to demand the full table d'hôte.

And if he refused? If he refused, what would any woman in Faith's situation do? Threaten him, with the most powerful weapon at her command. In her case the obvious, made-to-order threat would be one of exposure—stripping the veil from the phony research. By charging that he was party to the fraud, not merely a too-casual supervisor of the work of others, she could do him great injury. She would ruin her own career, but to someone being rejected by the man she saw as betraying her it might be worth self-destructing if she could drag him down with her.

Medea, I reminded myself, had killed her two precious sons to pay back their doublecrossing dad.

Maybe there'd been two showdowns that Saturday night— one with Barnard about the research, the other with Wells about becoming Mrs. Wells. If they had taken place in the order alleged by Barnard, Wells would have committed the murder.

—Unless after he'd gone, Barnard had been admitted to Faith's apartment a second time.

The bartender was back again. "Another Irish?" he said.

I roused myself. I didn't want my thinking to become muddled by drink. "I'll take the check."

When I stepped out onto the sidewalk I was almost directly crosstown from where I lived. I'd walk home and think some more on the way.

My rumination centered mainly on Wells. By the time I was passing St. Patrick's cathedral, I was focussing on an inconsistency. Wells had driven in from the country Monday evening (he said) and left the car parked in the street for a few minutes, leading to theft. When I was summoned to his office Tuesday morning and he asked me to try to find out what had happened to Faith, our conversation was interrupted by a call from the police. The message (again according to what Wells told me) was that the stolen articles—car radio and candlesticks—had been recovered.

My reasons for dwelling on this now were twofold. First, a conflict in dates. Barnard said he had seen Wells go into Faith's building on Saturday night, whereas Wells had spoken of being out of town until Monday. If Barnard's account was correct, the car could have been broken into prior to Monday night and the theft might have been reported earlier to the police. Proof on the police blotter that Wells had been in New York the night we believed Faith was murdered would certainly lend credence to the case against him.

And if an additional item, a power saw—not mentioned to me—had been stolen, the case would be even stronger.

Hadn't I heard Wells on the phone with the police officer, denying ownership of something that had been seized from the thief along with the candlesticks and radio? "No, that isn't mine," he said. "He must have got it somewhere else."

He wouldn't want the saw associated with him, even though he'd probably cleaned it off. A bit of bone or flesh, invisible to the naked eye though not to a microscope, might have stuck to it. . . .

Hazel was just home from work when I called to fill her in on the afternoon's developments.

153

"Ralph Wells?" She couldn't believe it at first, and for a moment I had the feeling that maybe I *had* gone overboard in my latest round of spitballing. But when I'd finished, she said, "It's still too much to take in—I see him as a nice, friendly person, always have—only after what you tell me I can't rule anything out."

Next morning Sanchez and Holsclaw were back in my apartment. They'd understood why I aborted the dramatic confrontation yesterday: after all, I'd told them how my suspicion of Barnard was first kindled by his ordering Tullamore Dew and they too had noticed the label on Wells's bottle. They agreed with me that this made *him* an immediate candidate for suspicion if not an actual suspect.

By now we were thinking in sync, and they were able to follow the reasoning that had led me to postulate that Wells might have killed and dismembered Frawley. I told them about the theft of the candlesticks and radio and had them wondering with me if it had taken place before Monday night . . . and whether something else might have been stolen from the car at the same time: the saw brought in from Bedford Hills.

Holsclaw used my phone to call the Manhattan precinct that included the block where Wells resided. Identifying himself as a member of the NYPD, he got someone to check the record for a complaint of theft by Wells on Tuesday morning. There was no such entry.

"How about Saturday, Sunday or Monday?" he asked as Sanchez and I sat silently by, me holding my breath.

"I see. And when the stuff was recovered, what did it include?"

He listened, his face impassive. "Mm. Thank you very much."

Despite what Sanchez had told me, Holsclaw enjoyed play-acting. Maybe he had just learned to enjoy it. Slowly, deliberately, he returned the phone to the cradle. Then he moved toward us, deadpan. Finally he said, "Wells called them Saturday night about being ripped off."

Saturday night!

Come on, come on—don't stop there! Finally I couldn't hold out any longer. "And what did they say was recovered?"

Now he permitted himself a grin. "Radio—candlesticks—and a power saw."

"Holy shit!"

Sanchez said, "As evidence, of course, that's purely presumptive. They have Wells' denial that the saw was his. And even if it was and it was stolen from his car, that doesn't prove anything about when or how he used it."

"Maybe not," I exulted, "but it convinces me that we've got the right guy for Frawley—and probably Dixon too! All we've got to do now is trap him!"

"That's all?" From Holsclaw.

"You know the sonofabitch is guilty and we know it," said Sanchez. "But it's going to take a hell of a lot more than this to make a murder charge stick!"

The voice of reality. "You're right of course," I acknowledged. The usual letdown that followed a high was setting in.

Suddenly I had an inspiration. Grisly, but that was what was required if we were going to shock Wells into a confession. "Look," I said. "I've got an idea. We buy another one of those Creuset casseroles—a big one. . . ."

I outlined what I had in mind. Holsclaw and Sanchez, who'd been primed to put on an act earlier to trap Barnard but been prevented, would now get their chance with Wells.

They approved of my plan.

We had some preparations to make. It was now Wednesday, and since Wells often got an early start to the country on Friday we agreed to aim for a Monday performance.

By now I really had to let Eve know what was cooking—so much had happened. I caught her at her hotel just as she was about to go to dinner. She was as shocked at the new developments as Hazel had been—or more so.

"Horrible!" she said. "Sick. I don't like you being in the middle of it. I wish I were there with you."

"Don't worry about me. I'll be all right." The words were spoken with more confidence than I felt.

But it was good to have somebody worrying.

EIGHTEEN

By Monday after lunch the three of us were assembled in my office, ready to strike. I had set up an appointment with Wells, ostensibly for myself alone. Let him be unprepared.

"One of us should walk in there wired," Sanchez informed me. "How about you?"

"Why me?"

Holsclaw answered. "Courts are always disallowing wires—cops overstepping the bounds—but you as a private citizen, maybe you stand a better chance."

"Okay."

Sanchez brought the little gizmo out of his pocket, I unbuttoned my shirt, he attached it. "Even if the court doesn't allow it, the guy's words on tape are a good thing to have. Can lead to a person making a deal.

"Don't forget your bag," Sanchez reminded Holsclaw as we were about to leave. In a big black plastic trash bag, cinched at the top with twine, was the surprise we were going to spring.

"Better tell Bert about Miranda," Hoslclaw said, picking the bag up off the floor.

"Oh, yeah. We can ask Wells questions, but if we arrest him we have to inform him of his right to remain silent."

"Right to remain silent, call his lawyer," I said. "I know Miranda."

"But unless he cracks when he sees our exhibit," Sanchez said, "we don't have grounds for arrest."

The police lab had done the obvious—checked the saw for traces of bone, blood or hair, and found nothing. Wells must have cleaned it with extreme care.

When our trio marched in on him, he looked only mildly

discomfited. "I didn't know I was being honored by your presence," he greeted the detectives. His eyes lingered on the outsize plastic bag Holsclaw was setting down on the floor. "Let me get another chair." He came around the desk, went into his secretary's office and slid one in. As he returned to his place, Holsclaw and I sat down. Before Sanchez took his seat, he closed the door even though there was no pair of secretarial ears out there at the moment.

Wells cleared his throat, waiting for someone to say something.

"We're back with some questions," said Sanchez.

"Sure. Any way I can help."

"That Saturday night . . . the one before the Monday Dr. Frawley didn't show up . . . were you here in the city?"

"Was I . . . ? Hm, let me think." He wrinkled his forehead. "Let's see. Normally I wouldn't be. No, I don't think I was. I would be at my place in Bedford Hills."

"You're sure about that?"

"Well. It's hard to be absolutely sure after all these weeks."

"Do you keep a journal?" asked Holsclaw.

"Not that would show where I was if I was following my usual routine. I note special things in the journal . . . meetings, professional affairs. Why are you interested in my whereabouts?"

Sanchez said, "One of your colleagues says you mentioned having driven into town that Saturday."

"Oh? Then I guess that's what I must have done. Who's the colleague?"

"We'll get to that. There's a record of your having called the Manhattan police the same night to report that your car was broken into."

"Then obviously I'm a bit fuzzy. Does it matter?"

"You also reported several things stolen: candlesticks, a radio and a saw . . . power saw."

"No!" He looked ready to do battle. "I said nothing about a saw!"

"Well, they recovered one with your other things," said Holsclaw. "The same thief admitted taking it."

"I went through all that with the police. Maybe the thief

didn't want to confess to two different thefts! It's not my problem!"

Sanchez turned toward Holsclaw. "Show Dr. Wells what you've got there."

Holsclaw leaned over, drew the trash bag closer and untied the twine. Reaching in with both hands, he carefully lifted out a suitcase. It was a near match to the two Fumi had inherited, but larger; I had found it in one of New York's best-stocked luggage shops. The canvas-like fabric was torn, water stained and further discolored by what might have been blood.

"This came out of the water," Holsclaw said. "And," unzipping it and removing a heavy object, "so did this." What he held out toward Wells was an orange-red Creuset casserole the next size up from Fumi's. Its lid was on; one might wonder if there was something inside.

We were all watching Wells's face. It showed only mild puzzlement.

"Do we have to tell you that the suitcase held this pot and parts of a female body?" said Sanchez.

Not horror, not guilt, but anger was Wells's visible reaction. "What is this? God damn it, what are you trying to pull?"

"You know what it is!" Sanchez accused, jumping up.

Wells also was on his feet. "You're trying to hang something on me! Whatever it is, charge me—or get the hell out!"

As I rose, he whipped around to me, eyes flashing. "You're behind this! You came to my place in the country, sucked up to me—making believe you were there to do me a favor! But you were trying to get something on me! Something to do with Faith? Is that supposed to be her suitcase? Her pot? Am I supposed to be her murderer? Christ!" He started to rush toward me, still breathing fire. "Don't think you're going to frame me! You've just lost your job!"

I remained where I was. After all, I had a couple of New York's finest to defend me. "You're not my employer, Dr. Wells," I said—loftily I hoped. My stomach was doing loop-the-loops.

He had stopped a foot away. "Get out! Get out!" Trembling with rage.

Holsclaw had retrieved the casserole and was stowing it

back in the suitcase and the suitcase in the bag. Sanchez left the room. Next, I sauntered out, Holsclaw trailing.

Brave words, mine: "You're not my employer . . ." But even if true, not necessarily relevant. Wells, going to Cromart who'd hired me, could cause me to join the ranks of the unemployed. And at my age, what were the prospects?

Would he, though? Would he be willing to risk having the whole situation involving him and Faith brought to light? Cromart or someone else just might listen to me even if Wells had made me the target of a smear.

I could only wait and see what he'd decide to do.

Out in the hall, Sanchez said, "Cool customer. I still think he's guilty as hell, but his cool is incredible. Most people on the spot like that would fall apart."

I said nothing. My trick, on which I'd staked all, had flopped.

"This is as far as we can take it," Holsclaw said. "Unless something else turns up."

He looked at me with what I felt was genuine concern.

"You know where to find us," said Sanchez, sounding like he really wished he could help. "Can he get you fired?"

"Probably," I said.

"Well, good luck."

Wouldn't it be that night that Doreen phoned from Toronto. An emergency.

"Paula's dance group has been invited to take part in a festival in Ottawa. Each person has to pay her own way. Transportation . . . three nights in a hotel. Meals. It comes to six hundred dollars and I just can't swing it. And it's so important to her! We have to let them know tomorrow."

I had my doubts about how important it was to Paula; I knew it was important to her mother, *prima ballerina frustrata.*

"This comes at a bad time," I said. "I may be losing my job."

"You what?"

She'd heard me all right; I could imagine what was running through her head. Bert loses job, Doreen loses income.

"I said I may be out of work."

"Why, what happened?"

"I antagonized a doctor here by practically accusing him
of murder."

"You're not serious."

"Very serious."

"Murder? What kind of a place you working at?"

"There's only been one other murder here in the last
month or so," I said.

"What makes you so sure he's guilty?"

"Oh, a saw that he sliced her up with. Conflicting statements about where he was when it happened. Scientific fraud
they were both party to—he and his victim. She was probably
going to spill the beans."

"If you're right about all that, how can he do anything
to you?"

"I know I'm right, the police know I'm right, but he— The
hell with it, Doreen. He's not in jail, he hasn't been indicted,
he may never be—and I'm the whistle blower. You know what
happens to them," I said, echoing Barnard.

"Is this the case you told Paula you were working on when
you were up here?"

"One of them."

"You had her walking on air . . . so proud, at last she had
something good she could tell her friends about you. So it
blew up in your face." This seemed to afford her a certain
satisfaction, perverse under the circumstances considering
how they could affect her. "Did you have to let him know you
suspect him?"

"Yeah . . . I did. We were trying to shock him into confess-
ing. I'm sorry to have to let Paula down, but—" I broke off.
"As a matter of fact, I'm not," I said. "Not sorry." I had
surprised myself. "She's only interested in her father for
what he can do for her: make her look good in front of her
friends—or pay for things. Maybe it'll do her good if it
doesn't work for once."

"That's a snide attitude. What about your monthly pay-
ments?"

"I'll manage those somehow. I'll pawn my jewels."

"She's going to be terribly disappointed about the festival.
All the other girls are going. How's it going to look?"

"Exactly what I was saying. If she wants me to explain it to her personally, I'll be glad to."

Hanging up, I felt better than I had since my none-too-glorious exit from Wells's office earlier in the day.

Eve still away, I called Hazel and gave her the scoop about the latest disaster—the episode immediately preceding that exit. She warned me not to take Wells's threat lightly; he'd probably work it out somehow to get rid of me in such a way that no one at Krinsky would listen to my side of the story, let alone believe it. Some misstep or incompetency, or—hardest of all to fight—personality defect would be attributed to me that would cost me my credibility.

Meanwhile, there was a murderer in our midst. "We've got to think of some way to catch him," Hazel said. "If we don't, there may be another body."

Yes, I thought. Mine.

The next afternoon, Tuesday, I answered my office phone and was almost absurdly grateful to hear Eve's voice.

"When did you get in?"

"About midnight. Flight was delayed. Is it safe to talk?"

I leaned to the side so I could just see around the door frame and assure myself that Altagracia was not listening in. Then I was ashamed; she'd earned my complete confidence. I said, "Go ahead."

"What's this about your being on the way out? Is it true?"

"I hope not. Who told you?"

"Deep Throat. No one you'd know. He wasn't free to tell me where he'd heard it."

"I've been warned I'll lose my job."

"By whom? No, don't say any more. Come to dinner tonight."

"Try to keep me away. Can I bring anything?"

"Just yourself."

Being together again was so pleasant that neither of us wanted to spoil it by getting down immediately to the evening's topic. So we drank and dined first. Yes, I was drinking. Michael wouldn't approve, but this was one of those times when I felt entitled.

Eve had changed her hairdo. Probably one of her husband's sisters had prevailed on her to eliminate the pile on top. And some had been cut off. She still looked good to me.

"I've missed you . . . missed this," I said. We were side by side on the sofa, having our coffee.

Eve set her cup down. "Now tell me what's been going on."

There was a lot to tell. I started at the point where I was picked up at the train station by Wells. The only place where I skipped something was when I got to the part about everybody going to Anthea's for tennis and Anthea coming on to me. If I weren't to lie about it I'd have to admit that we would have wound up on the bed except for my suspicion that I was being suckered.

God knows, there was enough to keep Eve riveted without that little sidebar.

"It's ghastly. It's unbelievable," she said at the end.

"But you do believe it?"

"I have to. And something's got to be done."

"I know. We can't just leave it at this."

"No, but we can't go off half-cocked either."

"I'm at sea at this point. I really don't know what to do next."

"It'll come to you. I'll think about it." She took my hand in hers. "I shouldn't have gone away when I did."

"How were we to know? Besides, it was part of your job."

"Well, I should've skipped Fort Worth. And now your job's in danger. —If Wells tries to get you fired. But it could play either way." I kissed her.

She kissed me back, then said, "Do you mind if I send you home?"

"I can't stay over?"

"I've had too much Texas hospitality, I have to recuperate. Tomorrow night you can take me out, if you want to. Then it's back to 'Your place or mine?'"

We stood and walked to the door. A good night kiss; she watched me down the hall till I turned the corner.

Tudor City is set apart from the regular Manhattan grid, built in a kind of horseshoe shape—though squared off. It's not a place you pass through on the way to somewhere else, so there is little traffic, vehicular or pedestrian. The very fact that no one else was in sight as I set off down the slope from Eve's toward Second Avenue should have caused me to be especially alert to danger. I wasn't thinking that way, however. So I was entirely unprepared when a figure suddenly lunged at me out of the dark. A man, Caucasian as far as my startled eyes could make out. The only thing that saved me from being mugged, or worse, was another man being pulled out of a doorway by a large German shepherd on a leash. Quick to spot trouble, the dog made a leap toward us, breaking loose. My would-be attacker instantly saw what was coming, turned and fled down the hill.

"Cauliflower!" cried the dog walker. "Cauliflower!" The fierce animal stopped in his tracks, going down on his haunches. He stared intently after the vanishing bad guy, his whole body shivering with thwarted aggression.

My inadvertent savior hurried over to me. Cauliflower (what a weird name!) trotted over to his side. "You almost got it!"

"Where did he come from? Suddenly he was on top of me." I felt dizzy.

"I should've let Max take care of him!" He patted the dog and rubbed his neck ruff. "No. Better I didn't. Sonofabitch could've had a gun—or a knife."

"Max?" I said stupidly. "I thought his name was Cauli-flower."

The man laughed. "That's code. A lot of us use code words—we don't want the wrong people giving commands."

I managed to muster what I could feel was a sickly grin. "Well, anyway, thank you for rescuing me."

"Thank Max."

"I do! Whatever the guy might have done to Max he could have done to me too. I owe this fellow a big juicy steak."

"Just doing his job."

I gave the beast a pat and was flattered when he gazed up at me and wagged his tail.

There are always people on Second Avenue and I was glad to join them and become part of the protective flow. As soon as I could I flagged down a cab. Second Avenue being a downtown thoroughfare, I had to start off in the opposite direction from Fifty-first Street, but it was worth the extra change to detour and reach home in one piece.

I had to wonder anew, as when Fumi was almost brained: was the attack one of those random things . . . me happening to start down the block when a street thug just happened to be looking for a score? Or was he particularly out to get Bertram W. Swain?

NINETEEN

At quarter to five the next afternoon Altagracia looked into my office and said Dr. Barnard wanted to see me.

"Tell him to come in."

He did, carefully shutting the door behind him. His manner was subdued but I sensed an underlying strain.

"What's up?" I asked, nodding toward a chair.

He settled onto it stiffly, holding himself tight. "You were going to find out if those detectives were planning to hassle me some more."

"Doesn't look like it. I think they're satisfied that Faith split because of the *Cell* article."

He leaned forward toward me and spoke in a low voice. "They're wrong. She didn't decide to go away. Something happened to her, and now I know what."

"Oh?"

"I can't tell you here. I could swear this whole place is bugged—things get around."

That was certainly true. The word that I was being fired, for example.

"Where shall we go?"

"Where the proof is. I have it at home."

"And why do you want to show it to *me*? If you've got proof, the police'll have to see it."

His agitation began to break through. "That's just the problem! Those detectives are out to get me. They'll twist everything—make it look like I'm involved." He got to his feet, gripped the back of the chair. "Between them and Wells . . . He's out to get me too! I don't know how to handle this. You've seen what's going on—I need your help before I go to the police!"

I was in a tug of war—intense curiosity versus caution. Could I trust this guy?

If I had to bet on either him or Wells being a murderer, my feeling now was that Wells was the more likely. But was this feeling a valid reason to accompany Barnard home, to find who knew what awaiting me?

Common sense said I was a fool to go with him. But having worked so hard to achieve a breakthrough, I knew I had to accept the challenge. If I was being maneuvered into a tight spot, I'd just have to rely on my ingenuity and my fists to get me out again.

I wished I'd taken better advantage of what Michael had to offer.

My ingenuity was already starting to operate: I saw a way to protect myself. If it worked.

"I'm supposed to be meeting someone for drinks," I said. "I'll have to cancel."

"Okay." Then, as I was about to pick up the phone he cast a nervous glance around the room. "But don't say where you're going!"

He watched as I lifted the phone from its cradle and punched three digits. Eve's extension rang. It rang again. Three rings, and then on the fourth . . . I got her answering machine. This morning I'd checked with her and confirmed that she'd recovered enough from her trip to come to work. But had she gone home a little early?

I now had to make another quick decision—whether to leave a message or to tell Barnard I was sorry, too late to cancel, and extricate myself from the whole deal.

I left the message: "This is Bert. Sorry I can't keep our five o'clock date. My Uncle Gene's just arrived in town and wants me to come over to his place right away. I'll try to talk to you later." I put a little emphasis on "try," hoping that if Eve heard the message in time to do something about it she'd figure out I wasn't sure what I was letting myself in for.

Last night after I walked into my apartment I'd started to phone her to tell her of the attempted attack. Then I thought better of it; at that point I didn't want her lying awake worrying about my safety. I'd skipped it this morning too. Now that I *wanted* her to worry I wished I'd prepared her by letting her know of the danger I'd escaped . . . a danger very possibly linked to the danger I might be getting into.

Please God she was still somewhere in the building! And if she was going to hear me, let it be within the next few minutes!

Gordon lived about ten blocks north of the medical center and suggested taking a taxi. I pleaded a headache, from being cooped up all day; and though it might have sounded a bit strange, since he was so eager to show me the evidence and I presumably was eager to see it, I said I really needed to walk. The fresh air would do me good.

Reluctantly he agreed.

I deliberately kept a slow pace, to give Eve more time. I could see my companion was itching to move faster. He asked after a couple of blocks, "Feeling any better?"

"A little." That was the extent of our conversation. He obviously didn't intend to tip his hand about what I'd be seeing and he was too tense to make small talk. I was trying to anticipate the surprise or surprises ahead but with no success. More than once I was convinced I was doing something dumb, but by now I felt fatalistic about it; the die had been cast, I was committed all the way.

He glanced at his watch several times. I wondered if he was on some kind of schedule. Probably he was supposed to be meeting Constance soon. The evidence, if it had just come into his possession, was making a demand on his time that he hadn't allowed for. And I was dragging my heels.

Well, good. Even if he wasn't the party guilty of murder, he still was too slick by half, a hot-eyed opportunist, and it was right that he should be uncomfortable.

We came to a stop before one of those gray stone houses with a marble stoop. To the left of the steps the front of the house curved, making for bay windows from bottom to top. "I'm on the second floor," said Gordon. "In the back."

We climbed to the heavy double front doors, glass and wrought iron. He unlocked the one on the right, then, using a second key, opened an interior, oak door with a pane in its upper half. The hall was dim and cool. A staircase rose along the right-hand wall; it was carpeted and had a carved newel post and balustrade, dark, probably mahogany. I judged the house to be pre-World War I and solidly built.

Following him up a flight, I was suddenly aware of my heart beating, loud in my ears. It almost seemed that Barnard must hear it. Breathing was an effort, my legs had gone weak. If I wouldn't have felt like an idiot, I would have turned and run.

Why should I care what I look like to him? I asked myself, toying with the possibility of escape. If I were on a plane about to take off and saw ice on the wings, would I go on sitting silent instead of yelling for the stewardess (pardon me, flight attendant)? Yes, I would no doubt go mute to my death rather than create a scene.

He had opened the door to his apartment by now and stood aside to let me pass.

Walking in from the foyer, I advanced to a good-sized living room. The exposure was to the north, and with venetian blinds tilted against the light, it was a bit dim but I could see that the furniture was Door Store-Workbench plain. I stopped, expecting Barnard to walk past me. I thought he would go open up the blinds. Instead, my wrists were suddenly seized from behind and jerked back. So it *was* a trap! I tried to break loose but the grip was like iron.

I did the only thing I could: kicked to the rear, hoping to connect with the most sensitive part of a man's anatomy.

Success! There was a groan of deep male anguish, and simultaneously my wrists were freed.

But as Barnard fell away, presumably grabbing his crotch, Wells emerged from the semi-dusk to my right. In one hand he held a piece of duct tape; I knew at once it was meant to cover my mouth. While I was still able to make a sound, I let out a loud "Help!" But it was the only chance I had, Wells slapping the tape across my lips as they came together again. Now it was a question of either stripping the tape off or fighting; Wells came at me with his fists and from the first blow to my cheek, which stunned and nearly felled me, I realized he was a formidable opponent. His getting me to spar in Bedford Hills was probably to give him some idea of my ability to defend myself in just such a situation as this. His weak performance would have been meant to deceive—

make me feel I was better than I was so I'd do something stupid, like letting Barnard con me into coming here. I was stunned not only by the physical blow he'd just landed, but by the emotional shock of having my worst suspicions about him confirmed. Most of what I'd been taught about boxing strategy flew out of my head. I punched with all the force I could summon, but hit mostly thin air, while Wells continued to pound flesh.

Now, from the side, Barnard dove for my ankles and brought me down on my back. Wells immediately knelt beside me, and again my wrists were the target. As I lay kicking and struggling to sit up . . . or turn . . . anything to wriggle loose, Barnard tossed his partner a length of cord. Cord *he* had meant to tie my wrists with—an action now carried out by Wells.

Then, my resistance limited to more kicking and writhing, Barnard and Wells together wrapped another length around my feet. After which, except for fruitless rolling around, I was effectively immobilized.

Finally I lay quietly, trying to muster my resources . . . if any. I was furious—furious with myself for not having seen the obvious without practically begging to have it forced on me. I should have guessed these two were in league with each other! *Of course* I had grown so threatening that now they were going to have to dispose of me.

Under Wells's self-congratulatory gaze and Barnard's cold, almost reptilian eyes, I had no way of expressing the hatred I felt, except by staring back at first one then the other.

"You left us no choice," Wells said quietly. "Our man almost took care of you last night. We can't afford another near miss.

"I made a mistake when I assigned you to find out what had happened to Faith. I thought it would look like I was doing something, and if you bungled the job it could make it harder for the police later."

"We had no idea you'd be so fucking persistent!" Barnard's tone almost made me feel that the plight I was in was all my fault.

"Gordon, he's worked so hard trying to figure things out," Wells said with unctuous solicitude, "don't you think we ought to tell him what really did happen?" At the younger man's nod he went on to enlighten me: "Faith and Gordon and I were all in on the little game of submitting that paper to *Cell*. And that's all it was—a game, beating somebody else by being faster and smarter."

"Like stealing a base," said Gordon.

"We didn't set out to trick anyone—we discovered there's a team at Stanford doing the same research we were, and if they got into print with it first . . . Gordon said it the other day, we were jumping the gun on something we were sure we could prove afterwards. And we knew we had a real contribution to make. More than the Stanford team.

"You've got to understand that by getting rid of a couple of obstacles we were freeing ourselves to continue studies that could benefit thousands . . ."

"Hundreds of thousands," amended Gordon, assuming his boss's sanctimonious tone. If I could only wipe that smirk off his face!

"I must say Faith didn't have much heart for it to begin with," Wells said. "She went along, mostly to strengthen her hold on me. She'd been wanting me to divorce Jessica and marry her. I told her that Jessica controlled the money in our house—what I earn is chicken feed—and she couldn't expect me to turn my back on that. Poor dear—Faith, I mean . . . she didn't realize the way the world works. She began to threaten to expose the research—even if it destroyed us all. I couldn't reason with her. Finally she demanded a showdown. Gordon and I agreed he should go see her first that night, to try to talk her out of it. And if that didn't succeed . . ."

It seemed to me I'd heard all I really needed to know, but if they had to keep going, it might at least prolong my life by a few minutes more. Still, it was crazy, their wanting to tell me everything. Like they had to justify themselves, and I was the only person they could ever do it with.

"Ralph brought his car—across the bridge from Queens."

"The hell with all these details!" interrupted Wells, suddenly impatient to get the show on the road.

"There's just one thing I'd like to know," said Gordon. "Those suitcases. Did they surface or did he figure out what we did and get the police to drag the river?"

"Forget it," Wells told him. "We'll never know unless we

remove that tape." To me he said, "You're so goddamned smart, you probably guessed we were responsible for Dixon too. He was a another threat—he was going to get lab space and funding that belonged to us. Once he was out of the way, we should have been safe against all comers. If it hadn't been for you.

"And Fumi," Gordon reminded him. "She's still a menace. She may not have doped it out yet . . . the missing suitcases, the casseroles . . . what they meant." I remembered her mentioning them in front of him when Faith's apartment was being cleared out. "But she knows about them. And when Bert here is found dead . . ."

"Yes," Wells agreed. "We've got to go after her again—and this time make sure it works."

"Trouble is," said Barnard, "if something happens to Fumi after Faith and Morgan Dixon, and now Bert, it's got to look suspicious."

"Maybe it can happen when Fumi's away somewhere," suggested Wells. "If we could get her out of town to a meeting . . ."

I had the odd sense that now they were forgetting I was present . . . a hopeful sense, almost. Perhaps their conversation would so absorb them that they'd leave me lying there while they went out and took a stroll through Central Park. But no; Wells addressed his next comment to me—a complaint: "There's something wrong with a system that puts pressure on scientists to take extra-legal measures. God knows we don't want to have to eliminate people!"

Poor Wells. *Poor* Barnard. After they disposed of me they were going to be *forced* to kill Fumi.

I wanted to scream, warn her. All that came of that was a gurgle in my throat.

Barnard was talking again. "In case you've been wondering, it may seem funny that Ralph and I are on good terms. I got a little upset there in his office with the detectives—it looked like if anything went wrong I was going to be the one . . ."

"Afterwards I made Gordon understand," Ralph said smoothly, "it was the only way to play the scene. As it turned out, no harm done."

Harm was about to *be* done—to me—and I wanted, and at the same time didn't want, to know how. Barnard, wiping sweat from his brow, then smoothing his mussed hair, obliged by answering the unasked question: "We've decided it's still a good idea for you to be killed by a mugger. At least that's what we'll make it look like. Late tonight we'll deposit you on a sidewalk somewhere in your neighborhood. People'll think you're drunk—or homeless—and walk around you. We'll have to mess up your clothes a little." He sounded almost apologetic.

Then, to show what a feeling person he was: "About me and Constance, I'm sure you're wondering whether I'm just taking advantage of her, or whether I really care. I wouldn't want you to go out with any false impression· I really do care."

I hadn't been wondering and I didn't give a shit whether he cared or not.

"Connie's a terrific girl," he added. "So you can rest your mind."

Rest my mind? My mind was in a tumult. I wasn't ready to say goodbye to life. I'd left all sorts of things undone, had done things I regretted and had never properly made up for. I wasn't nearly as attentive and responsible a father as I should have been; my troubles with Doreen had probably been as much my fault as hers. I'd been petty, I'd caused pain, I hadn't been a very good citizen—criticizing, complaining, sure, but not one to go around getting people's signatures on petitions. I hadn't marched in a demonstration about anything since Vietnam. I'd allowed my membership in Amnesty International and Public Citizen to lapse. I'd cultivated cheap cynicism. I'd been a pretty good son, I thought, but that was getting to be a long time ago, my parents were dead now. I'd almost lost track of my sister. As for other women, I'd danced a few around, taken what I wanted from them and then cast them aside. Well, not quite *cast* them, but either broken off with them on some lame excuse or not returned their phone calls. I hadn't read *Moby-Dick* all the way through (couldn't stay awake). I could never remember what hermeneutics were, or was, or what proleptic meant, or latifundia or rebarbative—even after I looked them up. I got food spots on new neckties. I think I sometimes had bad breath and inflicted it on lady friends. I still said lady, antagonizing worthy feminists. I hadn't got to know Eve well enough. I belched and farted a lot when I was alone, but in public pretended to be this well-bred individual. I ate meat, which involved raising animals under cruel conditions and killing them in painful ways (in spite of what we're told about humane methods). I passed by poor sods on the street (like I was about to become) that I should have given money to. I hadn't worked hard enough at being the writer I started out promising myself to be. Hell, I'd scarcely worked at it at all. I'd never learned anything about astronomy, and here we are under the great dome of heaven with all kinds of planetary things going on and changes of seasons and all that, and what do I know? What do I know about life? I've hardly begun to live it.

I was feeling pretty sorry for myself, not to say in great discomfort with that tape across my mouth and having to do all my breathing through my nose. It was a relief in a way to know it must mean the end when Wells picked me up under the arms, Barnard by the feet, and they laid me, face up, on a sofa.

Wells's hands loomed before my eyes, then descended to close around my throat. "It still doesn't seem right, having to kill people," he said. I struggled as his clutch tightened. My chest was exploding. . . .

I am swimming up to the surface. It's bright at the top; I strain toward the light. White light. It begins to be blinding. My lungs are about to burst. My arms and legs ache, unbearably, but I have to keep swimming, break through the crust of water.

I must have got through. The brilliant whiteness wavers, thins. A corner of a room, pale blue-white walls, shimmers into view. With it, someone bending down close to me. A face. Eve's.

Dear face.

"He's awake," she says to somebody. Then to me: "I got your message . . . 'Uncle Gene.' I called the cops. Just in time, poor darling."

My first day back on the job, Darryl Cromart asked me to come to his office. Although the silver-haired center director

173

kept one hand wrapped around the grip of a putter or something, he did me the courtesy of remaining seated for the whole of our brief interview. Still a little shaky, I started to apologize for not having been around to blunt the media onslaught triggered by the jailing of Drs. Wells and Barnard. Not that I could have if I *had* been. It seemed to me that as the man in charge during the period of the worst coverage in Krinsky annals, I was ripe for the fate Wells had planned for me—getting canned. It would be ironic if he still managed to accomplish that in spite of everything.

Instead, I heard: "This story had to come out—no one could have suppressed it. As it is, you've given the media a hero—Bert Swain, one of their own, That's going to be money in the bank for Krinsky for a long time."

Dr. Stokes sought me out in *my* office, to thank me for saving Constance from a disastrous marriage.

"How's she taking it?" I asked.

"Badly. No, I shouldn't say that. She's taking it as any young woman would who loved someone and thought he loved her, and then finds out . . . God, what a swine!"

I thought of saying, He really did care for her, in his way. He told me so. But I had an idea that any comfort this might provide would be very, very cold.

I hadn't felt up to phoning Paula while I was getting over the effects of my near-death experience. Tonight, however, warmed by the approbation of Stokes and Cromart—and Hazel who had gone out on a limb getting me hired—I felt restored enough to call Toronto.

Eve had cooked dinner at my place, to save me any unnecessary to-ing and fro-ing. When we got to the coffee I made the call.

Paula answered. Disappointed of course that I wasn't one of her school chums.

"Sweetie," I said, "remember the cases I told you about— the ones I was working on? One dead scientist, one missing?"

"Yes, but Mom says you didn't solve anything and you're probably going to lose your job." No wasted sympathy there.

"That isn't true any more. I've just helped the police catch the men who killed both people, and they're now in jail and my job is safe. If it isn't too late for that dance festival in Ottawa, I could still—"

"Daddy, you did that? Oh, wait till I tell!" The voice now sounded the way I always hoped for, accepting, approving. With her next words she lowered it, not to be overheard at her end. "I don't want to go to the dance festival! I never did!"

"May I?" It was Eve at my elbow, reaching for the phone. I passed it to her.

"Hello, Paula," she said. "Your dad's a hero. He's too modest to say so, but he did more than help the police. He solved the murders. And almost got killed himself. The police had to rescue him from the same two monsters—they had him bound and gagged and were strangling him. He was going to end up on the street, dead. I'm Eve by the way. I'm looking forward to meeting you."

When I got on the line again, Paula asked, "Is all that true?"

"Yep."

"Who's Eve?"

"I was about to tell you. Just the lady who called the police—saved my life."

"Something else! Tell her thanks! And how soon can you come see me again? My friends'll want to meet you! Or look—how about getting Mom to let me take a plane to New York? Like you were going to when you were here?"

"Great idea. Put your mother on."

It was arranged for the weekend after next.

After I rang off, Eve said, "I thought she ought to hear what her father's really like. From an unbiased source."

"Don't you think you may have exaggerated a little? That stuff about being a hero?"

"Stop putting yourself down. A fine upstanding man!"

I grinned lewdly and directed a glance to the area just below my belt. "How did you know?"

"Bertram Swain, I don't know what I'm going to do with you!"

"Yes you do," I said.

L'ENVOI

Hi, Doreen.

I've written a book! Maybe not the novel I was going to write, but the story you've just read. True crime.

Still, a book. It took me longer than I'd planned, but I've proved I can do it, from page one to

THE END

Have a nice day.